Michael Tucker

Everyman, I will go with thee, and be thy guide,
In thy most need to go by thy side.

This is No. 963 of Everyman's Library. A
list of authors and their works in this series
will be found at the end of this volume. The
publishers will be pleased to send freely to all
applicants a separate, annotated list of the
Library.

J. M. DENT & SONS LIMITED
10–13 BEDFORD STREET LONDON W.C.2

E. P. DUTTON & CO. INC.
286–302 FOURTH AVENUE
NEW YORK

EVERYMAN'S LIBRARY
EDITED BY ERNEST RHYS

FICTION

THE DIARY OF A NOBODY
BY GEORGE & WEEDON GROSSMITH
INTRODUCTION BY SIR JOHN SQUIRE

GEORGE GROSSMITH, born in London on 9th December 1847. Press representative, Bow Street Police Court, 1866–9, and intermittently to 1880. Entertainer with own sketches and songs from 1870. Leading figure in Gilbert and Sullivan operas, 1877–89. Died at Folkestone, 1st March 1912.

WEEDON GROSSMITH, born in London on 9th June 1854. Art student at R.A. Schools and Slade School. Comedy actor from 1885. Playwright. Died at London, 14th June 1919.

THE DIARY OF A NOBODY

GEORGE GROSSMITH

AND

WEEDON GROSSMITH

With illustrations
by Weedon Grossmith

LONDON: J. M. DENT & SONS LTD.
NEW YORK: E. P. DUTTON & CO. INC.

THE DIARY OF A NOBODY

originally appeared in *Punch*, and is re-published by permission of the publishers, Messrs. Bradbury and Agnew. The Diary has been since considerably added to. The excellent title was suggested by our mutual friend,

F. C. BURNAND,

to whom we have the great pleasure of dedicating this volume.

GEORGE GROSSMITH.
WEEDON GROSSMITH.

LONDON, *June* 1892.

INTRODUCTION

The Diary of a Nobody, the greater part of which originally appeared as a serial in *Punch*, was written by two brothers, of whom one was best known to the public as an actor and the other as an entertainer. No one ever thought of comparing them with Flaubert or Gissing, whom they very likely had not read, and the day of Tchekov had not yet arrived. Yet it is arguable that in point of mere realism of fiction they came as near to the truth as any of their more celebrated and more sombre contemporaries. It is true that their temperament gave their work a comic bias, as the temperaments of most of the "realists" gave theirs a gloomy bias. But if any man really wants what the critics used to call "a slice of life" here it is.

Naturally, there are qualifications. Mr. Pooter is slightly exaggerated, as are some of his companions, and an argumentative person with no sense of humour might well contest the above assertion by saying that Mr. Pooter would not even in a diary have so faith-fully recorded his extremest simplicities and his worst humiliations. But, whatever discounts may have to be made, the fact remains, as it seems to me, that a large area of English social life is painted in this book more faithfully and fully than anywhere else. Mr. Pooter does not beat his wife; nor do most Mr. Pooters. Mr. Cummings does not attempt to seduce her; nor would most of the Messrs. Cummings. Fifteen months pass without a murder or a divorce; there is no assault worse than the unpleasing trick played by Gowing when he made the whole party sit on the floor, no robbery worse than the abstraction of certain leaves from Mr. Pooter's diary, no debauch more reprehensible and disastrous than Mr. Pooter's excessive libations of champagne at the Lord Mayor's Ball. But fifteen normal months in a normal household would be equally free from extremes of human aberration and the worst malignities of Fate. It was the normal that our authors were depicting; they showed it in a comic light simply because they found it comic; thereby certainly coming nearer the hearts and minds of the Pooters themselves than do those other realists of the "Dull Monotony" school, who employ similar materials to exhibit a scene of utter tedium faithfully communicated to the reader.

The date is, shall we say, 1891; the site is Holloway, a typical suburb of the impecuniously respectable kind; the manners, customs, and experiences shown are those of the poorer middle classes in a London suburb of the late Victorian age. There are no set descriptions: everything is done, as it naturally would be in a diary, by an accumulation of little touches. We are given a picture of English social life, in a certain class, in a certain kind of place, and at a certain date. About the date the authors, doubtless, were not particular: they set down what were the facts when they wrote, and the mere lapse of time has given some of their details an historical value. The particular tone of the references to bicycling would in itself fix the date almost to a year: Cummings's paper on the superiority of the bicycle to the horse (but Lupin, who would now have a fast two-seater, preferred his smart little trap) and his lofty familiarity with the *Bicycling News* have the peculiar flavour of the nineties. There is something of the rose's beauty and transience about them now. Mrs. Cummings's songs, of which the most successful were *No, Sir,* and the *Garden of Sleep*, are also infallible indexes: a hundred years hence readers of the Diary will learn a good deal by looking up these two songs in the British Museum, unless by then that hospitable receptacle has burst its sides. "I bought a pair of stags' heads made of plaster-of-Paris and coloured brown": there is at once a record and a criticism; for amongst other things the Grossmiths were admirably sound on aesthetics, lampooning bad architecture, bad music, and bad furniture with equal certainty.

Those whose memories go back beyond 1914 will find an almost painful chasm about the reference to that quaint law—truly Victorian in its compromise and in the lies it led to—about *bona fide* travellers who could get drink out of hours on Sunday by the simple expedient of saying that they had come three miles. The Pooters' house and the decorations—fans, painted stools, etc.—of that and other houses date most emphatically. The house, "The Laurels," is drawn with ruthless power by Weedon; the square box covered with borrowed "features" out of scale with so modest a place; the stucco balustrade in front, the heavy steps to the porticoed front door, the weighty facings of the windows, the vast cornice with its unmeaning parapet atop, the puny shrubs in the front garden, the half-basement, the side door to the kitchen entrance, and behind all the telegraph wires and train smoke of an industrialism which had invaded the country at haphazards. These things, alas! we have still with us, and in myriads; houses do not pass so rapidly as clothes, slang, and people; but wherever we see such a house we know the period of it, it was built in the Pooters' lifetime. As diary and illustrations proceed we can almost define, though it is never mentioned, the precise smell of cooking that ascended from the Pooters' kitchen. The pictures of Pooter in the bath with the antiquated geyser, and of Pooter painting the washstand in the servant's bedroom, would alone tell us everything about his social status and habits.

Weedon Grossmith had the gift, which is shared by Mr. George Morrow, of drawing the commonest objects, jugs, railings, lamp-posts, gas-brackets, in such a way as to make them at once life-like, significant, and funny. His pictures reinforce a story which was in no need of reinforcement: and a whole way of life is recreated for us. What we are told suggests infinitely more: a whole world of people, before the age of motor-cars and jazz, living in the drabber London suburbs, the grand people in the larger villas, the Pooters and Cummingses in their plastered boxes, the tradesmen, the servants, the charwomen, the errand-boys. It is a mistake that no clergyman is introduced, but there is a wonderful tact about the intrusions of the larger and livelier world outside. The visits of Mr. Perkupp, the kind and prosperous master, of Mr.

Franching, of Mrs. James, a suburban quick to take up the latest fashionable fad; the glimpses of the glories of the Mansion House and the Volunteer Ball; the large air of the cultivated and statesmanlike Mr. Hardfur Huttle: these excitements come in just their right proportions. And though we may smile, looking backward and downward, at the things which the Pooters take seriously, we know in our hearts that we share their passions, and that we also have our toys and their dreams, in essentials like theirs:

Carrie's mother returned the Lord Mayor's invitation, which was sent to her to look at, with apologies for having upset a glass of port over it. I was too angry to say anything.

The Lord Mayor may not be what he was in the nineties; and even in the nineties there were quarters where his lustre did not shine so brightly as it did in Brickfield Terrace; but our laugh at the Pooters' little triumphs, vanities, and ambitions is in some measure a laugh at our own. "He [the curate] wants me to take round the plate, which I think a great compliment." The incident selected is selected with an exact eye to the effect, the delimitation of Mr. Pooter's sphere; but there again is a fact for the student of manners in ages to come, which is also a revelation of something to which neither time, place, nor class makes any difference. "It only shows how small the world is," on the other hand, is something, perhaps, which could only have become a standard remark in the middle class: the upper class being too consciously small, and the working class too large.

There are many enormous solemn books of great reputation in which the characters are no more surely drawn than they are here. Pooter's is the one full-length portrait: we know enough of him to deduce from it what he would say and do in any given situation; and it is a particular triumph of the authors that, although they make him so superbly silly, they leave us with an admiration of his "sterling worth." The presentiments of the others range, in point of scale, downwards until we come to the laconic Mr. Padge, who never says anything but "That's right," in a tone which makes us, as Mr. Belloc says, remember it all one's life. When has "economy of means" gone farther in the suggestion of character? "A vulgar-looking man," remarks the sober Mr. Pooter, "who appeared to be all moustache." He seized the most comfortable chair, blew out great clouds from his reeking pipe, and blandly contemplated the proceedings throughout the evening. The misadventure happened to Gowing:

I was so annoyed at the conduct of Padge, I said: "I suppose you would have laughed if he had poked Mr. Gowing's eye out?" to which Padge replied: "That's right," and laughed more than ever.

Next night:

Imagine my utter disgust when that man Padge actually came again, and not even accompanied by Gowing. I was exasperated, and said: "Mr. Padge, this is a surprise." Dear Carrie, fearing unpleasantness said: "Oh! I suppose Mr. Padge has only come to see the other Irving make-up." Mr. Padge cried: "That's right," and took the best chair again, from which he never moved the whole evening.

He rounds it off by saying "That's right," when Mr. Pooter is told by Burwin-Fosselton, the gifted imitator, to talk about what he understands. Weedon Grossmith's drawings of him, wedged into the best chair, with his shaggy moustache, his flat bald head, his perpetual pipe, his podgy hand, his vacuous, expectant face, perfectly develop the indications given. We know Padge; we can quite imagine him saying "That's right" when the malevolent Gowing said it would be quite the thing for him to present himself for an evening with the Pooters, who were total strangers to him; we are tempted to reconstruct his whole life, *ex pede Herculem* and the ichthyosaurus from a bone; we feel sure that he has retired from business and is a widower with a married daughter, who doesn't in the least know how much father is worth.

His introduction was a characteristic action of Gowing's, a selfish man, fond of Pooter, fond also of pulling Pooter's leg. The game of Mogul was Gowing's extremest action; but he appeared to great advantage after the Pooters had attained the dizzy heights of the Mansion House Ball, when:

He entered the room, without knocking, with two hats on his head and holding the garden-rake in his hand, with Carrie's fur-tippet (which he had taken off the downstairs hall-peg) round his neck, and announced himself in a loud, coarse voice: "His Royal Highness the Lord Mayor!" He marched twice round the room like a buffoon, and finding we took no notice, said: "Hulloh! What's up? Lover's quarrel, eh?"

That passage could not have been written without a very clear imaginative realisation of all the characters concerned. In the creation of minor characters the authors' invention is inexhaustible: they are always ready with a new one who is at once typical and yet strongly particularised. Lupin is a thousand "cards," yet he is Lupin. Mr. Cummings is a host of sedate bicycling—and rabbit-breeding, bowls playing, gardening, stamp-collecting—pioneers, yet he is Mr. Cummings with his own individual neutral tint.

And if the individuals are truthfully drawn, truths are also conveyed which transcend the experiences and idiosyncracies of individuals. Teddy Finsworth—who actually speaks almost as little as Mr. Padge—betrays a universal tendency when he meets Pooter again: "He insisted on my having a glass of wine (a thing I never do), and told me he lived at Middlesboro', where he was deputy town clerk, a position which was as high as the town clerk of London—in fact higher." The conversation about Pooter's dreams is almost horribly real. It concludes:

Carrie, who had hitherto been quiet, said: "He tells me his stupid dreams every morning nearly." I replied: "Very well, dear, I promise you I will never tell you or anybody else another dream of mine, the longest day I live." Lupin said: "Hear! hear!" and helped himself to another glass of beer.

Everyman and Everywoman are engaged here. Take, again, the conversation with the table-rapping Mrs. James:

Mrs. James said she thought I was very unkind, and if people were all as prejudiced as I was, there would never have been the electric telegraph or the telephone.

I said that was quite a different thing.

Mrs. James said sharply: "In what way, pray—in what way?"

I said: "In many ways."

Mrs. James said: "Well, mention one way."

I replied quietly: "Pardon me, Mrs. James, I decline to discuss the matter. I am not interested in it."

There is no burlesque in this; it happens, literally, a thousand times a day. The workings of Pooter's mind often have the same general applicability. After he has ruined Gowing's stick by enamelling it (an action particularly Pooterian) his entry is the entry any candid husband might make:

Purchased a new stick mounted with silver, which cost seven-and-sixpence (shall tell Carrie five shillings), and sent it round with nice note to Gowing.

It is akin to the entry of a few days later:

Franching called at office and asked me to dine at his club, "The Constitutional." Fearing disagreeableness at home after the tiff this morning, I sent a telegram to Carrie, telling her I was out to dine and she was not to sit up. Bought a little silver bangle for Carrie.

In passing it may be remarked that the selection of a club for Franching, who is so beautifully suggested both in text and illustration, shows that exquisite sense of fitness, and that fastidious care for detail, which are characteristic of these authors, whose scrupulosity is equalled by few professional writers.

I begin to feel that I am in danger of loading a light book with a ponderous introduction; but if I have imputed to the authors qualities and aims to which they gave no thought, I have imputed nothing to them which they did not possess or achieve. The lasting and growing popularity of the book a generation after its appearance and years after the deaths of the authors, is due I am convinced in part to its value as a record of fact as well as to the humour of its characterisation and invented incident. Commonly the two birds are killed with one stone. Take a typical entry of the sort of way in which the Pooter circle—such habits are not extinct, and can be paralleled in any class—would spend its evenings.

At supper young Mutlar did several amusing things. He took up a knife, and with the flat part of it played a tune on his cheek in a wonderful manner. He also gave an imitation of an old man with no teeth, smoking a big cigar. The way he kept dropping his cigar sent Carrie into fits.

That is nothing but a bare record of facts, in their order. They are funny because the human race is funny; we may find them additionally funny if in our time and circle the tricks are slightly different. Yet they are history. Some such record from ancient Greece would be cherished as an "illuminating document"; and while we are laughing at the Pooters and their friends we are also fascinated by the verisimilitude, the stark, unannotated realism of the events of the dialogue. The Grossmiths held the mirror up to nature, and there was a comic face in the glass. The exaggerated burlesques of their era are dead; their own transcript from life appears destined to a perennial popularity amongst the discriminating.

J. C. SQUIRE.

The following is a list of the works of the Grossmith brothers:

GEORGE GROSSMITH. *A Society Clown*, 1888: reminiscences. *The Diary of a Nobody*, 1894 (part author with Weedon Grossmith). *The George Grossmith Birthday Book*, 1904: a collection of original pieces, musical and otherwise. *Piano and I*, 1910: further reminiscences.

WEEDON GROSSMITH. *The Diary of a Nobody*, 1894 (part author and illustrator). *A Woman with a History*, 1896: a novel. *From Studio to Stage*, 1913: reminiscences. Among many plays, *The Night of the Party*, 1901, was his most successful.

CONTENTS

PAGE

WHY should I not publish my diary? I have often seen reminiscences of people I have never even heard of, and I fail to see—because I do not happen to be a " Somebody "—why my diary should not be interesting. My only regret is that I did not commence it when I was a youth.

CHARLES POOTER

The Laurels,
  Brickfield Terrace,
    Holloway.

WE SETTLE DOWN IN OUR NEW HOME,
AND I RESOLVE TO KEEP A DIARY.
TRADESMEN TROUBLE US A BIT, SO DOES
THE SCRAPER.   THE CURATE CALLS AND
PAYS ME A GREAT COMPLIMENT.

CHAPTER I

My dear wife Carrie and I have just been a week in our new house, "The Laurels," Brickfield Terrace, Holloway — a nice six-roomed residence, not counting basement, with a front breakfast-parlour. We have a little front garden; and there is a flight of ten steps up to the front door, which, by-the-by, we keep locked with the chain up. Cummings, Gowing, and our other intimate friends always come to the little side entrance, which saves the servant the trouble of going up to the front door, thereby taking her from her work. We have a nice little back garden which runs down to the railway. We were rather afraid of the noise of the trains at first, but the landlord said we should not notice them after a bit, and took £2 off the rent. He was certainly right; and beyond the cracking of the garden wall at the bottom, we have suffered no inconvenience.

After my work in the City, I like to be at home. What's the good of a home, if you are never in it? "Home, Sweet Home," that's my motto. I am always in of an evening. Our old friend Gowing may drop in without ceremony; so may Cummings, who lives opposite. My dear wife

27

" The Laurels."

Caroline and I are pleased to see them, if they like to drop in on us. But Carrie and I can manage to pass our evenings together without friends. There is always something to be done : a tin-tack here, a Venetian blind to put straight, a fan to nail up, or part of a carpet to nail down—all of which I can do with my pipe in my mouth ; while Carrie is not above putting a button on a shirt, mending a pillow-case, or practising the " Sylvia Gavotte " on our new cottage piano (on the three years' system), manufactured by W. Bilkson (in small letters), from Collard and Collard (in very large letters). It is also a great comfort to us to know that our boy Willie is getting on so well in the Bank at Oldham. We should like to see more of him. Now for my diary :—

April 3. Tradesmen called for custom, and I promised Farmerson, the ironmonger, to give him a turn if I wanted any nails or tools. By-the-by, that reminds me there is no key to our bedroom door, and the bells must be seen to. The parlour bell is broken, and the front door rings up in the servant's bedroom, which is ridiculous. Dear friend Gowing dropped in, but wouldn't stay, saying there was an infernal smell of paint.

April 4. Tradesmen still calling : Carrie being out, I arranged to deal with Horwin, who seemed a civil butcher with a nice clean shop. Ordered a shoulder of mutton for

W.G.

Our dear friend Gowing.

to-morrow, to give him a trial. Carrie arranged with Borset, the butterman, and ordered a pound of fresh butter, and a pound and a half of salt ditto for kitchen, and a shilling's worth of eggs. In the evening, Cummings unexpectedly dropped in to show me a meerschaum pipe he had won in a raffle in the City, and told me to handle it carefully, as it would spoil the colouring if the hand was moist. He said he wouldn't stay, as he didn't care much for the smell of the paint, and fell over the scraper as he went out. Must get the scraper removed, or else I shall get into a *scrape*. I don't often make jokes.

April 5. Two shoulders of mutton arrived, Carrie having arranged with another butcher without consulting me. Gowing called, and fell over scraper coming in. *Must* get that scraper removed.

April 6. Eggs for breakfast simply shocking; sent them back to Borset with my compliments, and he needn't call any more for orders. Couldn't find umbrella, and though it was pouring with rain, had to go without it. Sarah said Mr. Gowing must have took it by mistake last night, as there was a stick in the 'all that didn't belong to nobody. In the evening, hearing someone talking in a loud voice to the servant in the downstairs hall, I went out to see who it was, and was surprised to find it was Borset, the butterman, who was both drunk and offensive.

W. G.

Our dear friend Cummings.

Borset, on seeing me, said he would be hanged if he would ever serve City clerks any more—the game wasn't worth the candle. I restrained my feelings, and quietly remarked that I thought it was *possible* for a City clerk to be a *gentleman*. He replied he was very glad to hear it, and wanted to know whether I had ever come across one, for *he* hadn't. He left the house, slamming the door after him, which nearly broke the fanlight; and I heard him fall over the scraper, which made me feel glad I hadn't removed it. When he had gone, I thought of a splendid answer I ought to have given him. However, I will keep it for another occasion.

April 7. Being Saturday, I looked forward to being home early, and putting a few things straight; but two of our principals at the office were absent through illness, and I did not get home till seven. Found Borset waiting. He had been three times during the day to apologise for his conduct last night. He said he was unable to take his Bank Holiday last Monday, and took it last night instead. He begged me to accept his apology, and a pound of fresh butter. He seems, after all, a decent sort of fellow; so I gave him an order for some fresh eggs, with a request that on this occasion they *should* be fresh. I am afraid we shall have to get some new stair-carpets after all; our old ones are not quite wide enough to meet the paint on either side. Carrie suggests that we might ourselves broaden

B

the paint. I will see if we can match the colour (dark chocolate) on Monday.

April 8, *Sunday*. After Church, the Curate came back with us. I sent Carrie in to open front door, which we do not use except on special occasions. She could not get it open, and after all my display, I had to take the Curate (whose name, by-the-by, I did not catch) round the side entrance. He caught his foot in the scraper, and tore the bottom of his trousers. Most annoying, as Carrie could not well offer to repair them on a Sunday. After dinner, went to sleep. Took a walk round the garden, and discovered a beautiful spot for sowing mustard-and-cress and radishes. Went to Church again in the evening : walked back with the Curate. Carrie noticed he had got on the same pair of trousers, only repaired. He wants me to take round the plate, which I think a great compliment.

TRADESMEN AND THE SCRAPER STILL TROUBLESOME. GOWING RATHER TIRESOME WITH HIS COMPLAINTS OF THE PAINT. I MAKE ONE OF THE BEST JOKES OF MY LIFE. DELIGHTS OF GARDENING. MR. STILLBROOK, GOWING, CUMMINGS, AND I HAVE A LITTLE MISUNDERSTANDING. SARAH MAKES ME LOOK A FOOL BEFORE CUMMINGS.

CHAPTER II

April 9.

COMMENCED the morning badly. The butcher, whom we decided *not* to arrange with, called and blackguarded me in the most uncalled-for manner. He began by abusing me, and saying he did not want my custom. I simply said : "Then what are you making all this fuss about it for?" And he shouted out at the top of his voice, so that all the neighbours could hear : "Pah! go along. Ugh! I could buy up ' things ' like you by the dozen! "

I shut the door, and was giving Carrie to understand that this disgraceful scene was entirely her fault, when there was a violent kicking at the door, enough to break the panels. It was the blackguard butcher again, who said he had cut his foot over the scraper, and would immediately bring an action against me. Called at Farmerson's, the ironmonger, on my way to town, and gave him the job of moving the scraper and repairing the bells, thinking it scarcely worth while to trouble the landlord with such a trifling matter.

Arrived home tired and worried. Mr. Putley, a painter and decorator, who had sent in a card, said he could not match the colour on the stairs, as it contained Indian carmine. He said he spent half-a-day calling at warehouses to see if he could get it. He suggested he should entirely repaint the stairs. It would cost very little more ; if he tried to match it, he could only make a bad job of it. It would be more satisfactory to him and to us to have the work done properly. I consented, but felt I had been talked over. Planted some mustard-and-cress and radishes, and went to bed at nine.

April 10. Farmerson came round to attend to the scraper himself. He seems a very civil fellow. He says he does not usually conduct such small jobs personally, but for *me* he would do so. I thanked him, and went to town. It is disgraceful how late some of the young clerks are at arriving. I told three of them that if Mr. Perkupp, the principal, heard of it, they might be discharged.

Pitt, a monkey of seventeen, who has only been with us six weeks, told me " to keep my hair on ! " I informed him I had had the honour of being in the firm twenty years, to which he insolently replied that I " looked it." I gave him an indignant look, and said : " I demand from you some respect, sir." He replied : " All right, go on demanding." I would not argue with him any further. You cannot argue with people like that. In the evening Gowing called, and repeated his complaint about the smell of paint. Gowing is sometimes very tedious with his remarks, and not always cautious ; and Carrie once very properly reminded him that she was present.

Mustard-and-cress and radishes not
April 11. come up yet. To-day was a day of
annoyances. I missed the quarter-to-
nine 'bus to the City, through having words with
the grocer's boy, who for the second time had the
impertinence to bring his basket to the hall-door,
and had left the marks of his dirty boots on the
fresh-cleaned door-steps. He said he had knocked
at the side door with his knuckles for a quarter
of an hour. I knew Sarah, our servant, could
not hear this, as she was upstairs doing the bed-
rooms, so asked the boy why he did not ring the
bell ? He replied that he did pull the bell, but
the handle came off in his hand.

I was half-an-hour late at the office, a thing
that has never happened to me before. There
has recently been much irregularity in the
attendance of the clerks, and Mr. Perkupp, our
principal, unfortunately chose this very morning
to pounce down upon us early. Someone had
given the tip to the others. The result was that
I was the only one late of the lot. Buckling,
one of the senior clerks, was a brick, and I was
saved by his intervention. As I passed by Pitt's
desk, I heard him remark to his neighbour :
" How disgracefully late some of the head clerks
arrive ! " This was, of course, meant for me. I
treated the observation with silence, simply giving
him a look, which unfortunately had the effect
of making both of the clerks laugh. Thought
afterwards it would have been more dignified if I
had pretended not to have heard him at all.

Cummings called in the evening, and we played dominoes.

April 12.   Mustard-and-cress and radishes not come up yet. Left Farmerson repairing the scraper, but when I came home found three men working. I asked the meaning of it, and Farmerson said that in making a fresh hole he had penetrated the gas-pipe. He said it was a most ridiculous place to put the gas-pipe, and the man who did it evidently knew nothing about his business. I felt his excuse was no consolation for the expense I shall be put to.

In the evening, after tea, Gowing dropped in, and we had a smoke together in the breakfast-parlour. Carrie joined us later, but did not stay long, saying the smoke was too much for her. It was also rather too much for me, for Gowing had given me what he called a green cigar, one that his friend Shoemach had just brought over from America. The cigar didn't look green, but I fancy I must have done so; for when I had smoked a little more than half I was obliged to retire on the pretext of telling Sarah to bring in the glasses.

I took a walk round the garden three or four times, feeling the need of fresh air. On returning Gowing noticed I was not smoking : offered me another cigar, which I politely declined. Gowing began his usual sniffing, so, anticipating him, I said : " You're not going to complain of the smell of paint again ? " He said : " No, not this time ;

but I'll tell you what, I distinctly smell dry rot."
I don't often make jokes, but I replied : "You're
talking a lot of *dry rot* yourself." I could not help
roaring at this, and Carrie said her sides quite
ached with laughter. I never was so immensely
tickled by anything I had ever said before. I
actually woke up twice during the night, and
laughed till the bed shook.

An extraordinary coincidence : Carrie
April 13. had called in a woman to make some
chintz covers for our drawing-room
chairs and sofa to prevent the sun fading the
green rep of the furniture. I saw the woman,
and recognised her as a woman who used to work
years ago for my old aunt at Clapham. It only
shows how small the world is.

Spent the whole of the afternoon in
April 14. the garden, having this morning picked
up at a bookstall for fivepence a
capital little book, in good condition, on *Gardening*.
I procured and sowed some half-hardy annuals
in what I fancy will be a warm, sunny border.
I thought of a joke, and called out Carrie. Carrie
came out rather testy, I thought. I said : "I
have just discovered we have got a lodging-house."
She replied : "How do you mean ?" I said :
"Look at the *boarders*." Carrie said : "Is that
all you wanted me for ?" I said : "Any other
time you would have laughed at my little
pleasantry." Carrie said : "Certainly—*at any*

Stillbrook lags behind. Going up hill.

Going down hill.

other time, but not when I am busy in the house."
The stairs look very nice. Gowing called, and
said the stairs looked *all right*, but it made the
banisters look *all wrong*, and suggested a coat of
paint on them also, which Carrie quite agreed
with. I walked round to Putley, and fortunately
he was out, so I had a good excuse to let the
banisters slide. By-the-by, that is rather funny.

April 15,
Sunday.
At three o'clock Cummings and
Gowing called for a good long walk
over Hampstead and Finchley, and
brought with them a friend named
Stillbrook. We walked and chatted together,
except Stillbrook, who was always a few yards
behind us staring at the ground and cutting at the
grass with his stick.

As it was getting on for five, we four held a
consultation, and Gowing suggested that we
should make for " The Cow and Hedge " and get
some tea. Stillbrook said : " A brandy-and-soda
was good enough for him." I reminded them that
all public-houses were closed till six o'clock.
Stillbrook said, " That's all right — *bona-fide*
travellers."

We arrived ; and as I was trying to pass, the man
in charge of the gate said : " Where from ? " I
replied : " Holloway." He immediately put up
his arm, and declined to let me pass. I turned
back for a moment, when I saw Stillbrook, closely
followed by Cummings and Gowing, make for the
entrance. I watched them, and thought I would

Nearly there.

have a good laugh at their expense. I heard the porter say : " Where from ? " When, to my surprise, in fact disgust, Stillbrook replied : " Blackheath," and the three were immediately admitted.

Gowing called to me across the gate, and said : " We shan't be a minute." I waited for them the best part of an hour. When they appeared they were all in most excellent spirits, and the only one who made an effort to apologise was Mr. Stillbrook, who said to me : " It was very rough on you to be kept waiting, but we had another spin for S. and B.'s." I walked home in silence ; I couldn't speak to them. I felt very dull all the evening, but deemed it advisable *not* to say anything to Carrie about the matter.

April 16. After business, set to work in the garden. When it got dark I wrote to Cummings and Gowing (who neither called, for a wonder ; perhaps they were ashamed of themselves) about yesterday's adventure at " The Cow and Hedge." Afterwards made up my mind not to write *yet*.

April 17. Thought I would write a kind little note to Gowing and Cummings about last Sunday, and warning them against Mr. Stillbrook. Afterwards, thinking the matter over, tore up the letter and determined not to *write* at all, but to *speak* quietly to them. Dumbfounded at receiving a sharp letter from

Cummings, saying that both he and Gowing had been waiting for an explanation of *my* (mind you, MY) extraordinary conduct coming home on Sunday. At last I wrote : " I thought I was the aggrieved party ; but as I freely forgive you, you — feeling yourself aggrieved — should bestow forgiveness on me." I have copied this *verbatim* in the diary, because I think it is one of the most perfect and thoughtful sentences I have ever written. I posted the letter, but in my own heart I felt I was actually apologising for having been insulted.

April 18. Am in for a cold. Spent the whole day at the office sneezing. In the evening, the cold being intolerable, sent Sarah out for a bottle of Kinahan. Fell asleep in the arm-chair, and woke with the shivers. Was startled by a loud knock at the front door. Carrie awfully flurried. Sarah still out, so went up, opened the door, and found it was only Cummings. Remembered the grocer's boy had again broken the side-bell. Cummings squeezed my hand, and said : " I've just seen Gowing. All right. Say no more about it." There is no doubt they are both under the impression I have apologised.

While playing dominoes with Cummings in the parlour, he said : " By-the-by, do you want any wine or spirits ? My cousin Merton has just set up in the trade, and has a splendid whisky, four years in bottle, at thirty-eight shillings. It is

"Please, sir, the grocer says he ain't got no more Kinahan,
but you'll find this very good at two-and-six."

worth your while laying down a few dozen of it."
I told him my cellars, which were very small, were
full up. To my horror, at that very moment, Sarah
entered the room, and putting a bottle of whisky,
wrapped in a dirty piece of newspaper, on the table
in front of us, said : " Please, sir, the grocer says
he ain't got no more Kinahan, but you'll find this
very good at two-and-six, with twopence returned
on the bottle ; and, please, did you want any more
sherry ? as he has some at one-and-three, as dry
as a nut ! "

A CONVERSATION WITH MR. MERTON ON
SOCIETY. MR. AND MRS. JAMES, OF
SUTTON, COME UP. A MISERABLE EVENING
AT THE TANK THEATRE. EXPERIMENTS
WITH ENAMEL PAINT. I MAKE ANOTHER
GOOD JOKE ; BUT GOWING AND CUMMINGS
ARE UNNECESSARILY OFFENDED. I PAINT
THE BATH RED, WITH UNEXPECTED RESULT.

CHAPTER III

CUMMINGS called, bringing with him
April 19. his friend Merton, who is in the wine
trade. Gowing also called. Mr.
Merton made himself at home at once, and Carrie
and I were both struck with him immediately,
and thoroughly approved of his sentiments.

He leaned back in his chair and said : " You
must take me as I am ; " and I replied : " Yes—
and you must take us as we are. We're homely
people, we are not swells."

He answered : " No, I can see that," and
Gowing roared with laughter ; but Merton in a
most gentlemanly manner said to Gowing : " I
don't think you quite understand me. I intended
to convey that our charming host and hostess were
superior to the follies of fashion, and preferred
leading a simple and wholesome life to gadding
about to twopenny-halfpenny tea-drinking after-
noons, and living above their incomes."

I was immensely pleased with these sensible
remarks of Merton's, and concluded that subject
by saying : " No, candidly, Mr. Merton, we don't
go into Society, because we do not care for it ;
and what with the expense of cabs here and cabs
there, and white gloves and white ties, etc., it
doesn't seem worth the money."

Merton said in reference to *friends :* " My
motto is ' Few and True ; ' and, by the way, I also

apply that to wine, ' Little and Good.' " Gowing
said : " Yes, and sometimes ' cheap and tasty,'
eh, old man ? " Merton, still continuing, said he
should treat me as a friend, and put me down for a
dozen of his " Lockanbar " whisky, and as I was
an old friend of Gowing, I should have it for 36s.,
which was considerably under what he paid for it.

He booked his own order, and further said that
at any time I wanted any passes for the theatre I
was to let him know, as his name stood good for
any theatre in London.

April 20. Carrie reminded me that as her old
school friend, Annie Fullers (now
Mrs. James), and her husband had
come up from Sutton for a few days, it would look
kind to take them to the theatre, and would I drop
a line to Mr. Merton asking him for passes for
four, either for the Italian Opera, Haymarket, Savoy,
or Lyceum. I wrote Merton to that effect.

April 21. Got a reply from Merton, saying he
was very busy, and just at present
couldn't manage passes for the Italian
Opera, Haymarket, Savoy, or Lyceum, but the
best thing going on in London was the *Brown
Bushes*, at the Tank Theatre, Islington, and
enclosed seats for four ; also bill for whisky.

April 23. Mr. and Mrs. James (Miss Fullers
that was) came to meat-tea, and we
left directly after for the Tank
Theatre. We got a 'bus that took us to King's

Cross, and then changed into one that took us to the " Angel." Mr. James each time insisted on paying for all, saying that I had paid for the tickets and that was quite enough.

We arrived at theatre, where, curiously enough, all our 'bus-load except an old woman with a basket seemed to be going in. I walked ahead and presented the tickets. The man looked at them, and called out : " Mr. Willowly ! do you know anything about these ? " holding up my tickets. The gentleman called to came up and examined my tickets, and said : " Who gave you these ? " I said, rather indignantly : " Mr. Merton, of course." He said : " Merton ? Who's he ? " I answered, rather sharply : " You ought to know, his name's good at any theatre in London." He replied : " Oh ! is it ? Well, it ain't no good here. These tickets, which are *not* dated, were issued under Mr. Swinstead's management, which has since changed hands." While I was having some very unpleasant words with the man, James, who had gone upstairs with the ladies, called out : " Come on ! " I went up after them, and a very civil attendant said : " This way, please, box H." I said to James : " Why, how on earth did you manage it ? " and to my horror he replied : " Why, paid for it of course."

This was humiliating enough, and I could scarcely follow the play, but I was doomed to still further humiliation. I was leaning out of the box, when my tie—a little black bow which fastened on to the stud by means of a new patent—fell into the pit below. A clumsy man not noticing it, had his foot on it for ever so long before he discovered it. He then picked it up and eventually flung it under the next seat in disgust. What with the box incident and the tie, I felt quite miserable. Mr. James, of Sutton, was very good. He said: "Don't worry—no one will notice it with your beard. That is the only advantage of growing one that I can see." There was no occasion for that remark, for Carrie is very proud of my beard.

To hide the absence of the tie I had to keep my chin down the rest of the evening, which caused a pain at the back of my neck.

April 24. Could scarcely sleep a wink through thinking of having brought up Mr. and Mrs. James from the country to go to the theatre last night, and his having paid for a private box because our order was not honoured; and such a poor play too. I wrote a very satirical letter to Merton, the wine merchant, who gave us the pass, and said, "Considering we had to *pay* for our seats, we did our *best* to appreciate the performance." I thought this line rather cutting, and I asked Carrie how many p's there were in appreciate, and she said "One." After I sent off the letter I looked at the dictionary and found there were two. Awfully vexed at this.

Decided not to worry myself any more about the James's; for, as Carrie wisely said, "We'll make it all right with them by asking them up from Sutton one evening next week to play at Bézique."

In consequence of Brickwell telling
April 25. me his wife was working wonders
with the new Pinkford's enamel paint,
I determined to try it. I bought two tins of red
on my way home. I hastened through tea, went
into the garden and painted some flower-pots.
I called out Carrie, who said : " You've always
got some new-fangled craze ; " but she was
obliged to admit that the flower-pots looked
remarkably well. Went upstairs into the servant's
bedroom and painted her washstand, towel-horse,
and chest of drawers. To my mind it was an
extraordinary improvement, but as an example of
the ignorance of the lower classes in the matter
of taste, our servant, Sarah, on seeing them,
evinced no sign of pleasure, but merely said " she
thought they looked very well as they was before."

Got some more red enamel paint
April 26. (red, to my mind, being the best
colour), and painted the coal-scuttle,
and the backs of our *Shakespeare*, the binding of
which had almost worn out.

Painted the bath red, and was
April 27. delighted with the result. Sorry to
say Carrie was not, in fact we had a
few words about it. She said I ought to have
consulted her, and she had never heard of such a
thing as a bath being painted red. I replied :
" It's merely a matter of taste."
Fortunately, further argument on the subject

I painted the washstand in the servant's bedroom.

was stopped by a voice saying, " May I come in ? "
It was only Cummings, who said, " Your maid
opened the door, and asked me to excuse her
showing me in, as she was wringing out some
socks." I was delighted to see him, and suggested
we should have a game of whist with a dummy,
and by way of merriment said : " *You* can be the
dummy." Cummings (I thought rather ill-
naturedly) replied : " Funny as usual." He said
he couldn't stop, he only called to leave me the
Bicycle News, as he had done with it.

Another ring at the bell; it was Gowing, who
said he " must apologise for coming so often, and
that one of these days *we* must come round to
him." I said : " A very extraordinary thing has
struck me." "Something funny, as usual," said
Cummings. "Yes," I replied ; " I think even
you will say so this time. It's concerning you
both ; for doesn't it seem odd that Gowing's
always *coming* and Cummings' always *going* ? "
Carrie, who had evidently quite forgotten about
the bath, went into fits of laughter, and as for
myself, I fairly doubled up in my chair, till it
cracked beneath me. I think this was one of the
best jokes I have ever made.

Then imagine my astonishment on perceiving
both Cummings and Gowing perfectly silent,
and without a smile on their faces. After rather
an unpleasant pause, Cummings, who had opened
a cigar-case, closed it up again and said : " Yes—
I think, after that, I *shall* be going, and I am sorry
I fail to see the fun of your jokes." Gowing said

he didn't mind a joke when it wasn't rude, but a pun on a name, to his thinking, was certainly a little wanting in good taste. Cummings followed it up by saying, if it had been said by anyone else but myself, he shouldn't have entered the house again. This rather unpleasantly terminated what might have been a cheerful evening. However, it was as well they went, for the charwoman had finished up the remains of the cold pork.

April 28. At the office, the new and very young clerk Pitt, who was very impudent to me a week or so ago, was late again. I told him it would be my duty to inform Mr. Perkupp, the principal. To my surprise, Pitt apologised most humbly and in a most gentlemanly fashion. I was unfeignedly pleased to notice this improvement in his manner towards me, and told him I would look over his unpunctuality. Passing down the room an hour later, I received a smart smack in the face from a rolled-up ball of hard foolscap. I turned round sharply, but all the clerks were apparently riveted to their work. I am not a rich man, but I would give half-a-sovereign to know whether that was thrown by accident or design. Went home early and bought some more enamel paint—black this time—and spent the evening touching up the fender, picture-frames, and an old pair of boots, making them look as good as new. Also painted Gowing's walking-stick, which he left behind, and made it look like ebony.

I looked like Marat in the bath, in Madame Tussaud's.

April 29, *Sunday*. Woke up with a fearful headache and strong symptoms of a cold. Carrie, with a perversity which is just like her, said it was " painter's colic," and was the result of my having spent the last few days with my nose over a paint-pot. I told her firmly that I knew a great deal better what was the matter with me than she did. I had got a chill, and decided to have a bath as hot as I could bear it. Bath ready—could scarcely bear it so hot. I persevered, and got in ; very hot, but very acceptable. I lay still for some time.

On moving my hand above the surface of the water, I experienced the greatest fright I ever received in the whole course of my life ; for imagine my horror on discovering my hand, as I thought, full of blood. My first thought was that I had ruptured an artery, and was bleeding to death, and should be discovered, later on, looking like a second Marat, as I remember seeing him in Madame Tussaud's. My second thought was to ring the bell, but remembered there was no bell to ring. My third was, that there was nothing but the enamel paint, which had dissolved with boiling water. I stepped out of the bath, perfectly red all over, resembling the Red Indians I have seen depicted at an East-End theatre. I determined not to say a word to Carrie, but to tell Farmerson to come on Monday and paint the bath white.

THE BALL AT THE MANSION HOUSE.

CHAPTER IV

PERFECTLY astounded at receiving an invitation for Carrie and myself from the Lord and Lady Mayoress to the Mansion House, to " meet the Representatives of Trades and Commerce." My heart beat like that of a schoolboy's. Carrie and I read the invitation over two or three times. I could scarcely eat my breakfast. I said—and I felt it from the bottom of my heart,—" Carrie darling, I was a proud man when I led you down the aisle of the church on our wedding day ; that pride will be equalled, if not surpassed, when I lead my dear, pretty wife up to the Lord and Lady Mayoress at the Mansion House." I saw the tears in Carrie's eyes, and she said : " Charlie dear, it is I who have to be proud of you. And I am very, very proud of you. You have called me pretty ; and as long as I am pretty in your eyes, I am happy. You, dear old Charlie, are *not* handsome, but you are *good*, which is far more noble." I gave her a kiss, and she said : " I wonder if there will be any dancing ? I have not danced with you for years."

April 30.

I cannot tell what induced me to do it, but I seized her round the waist, and we were silly enough to be executing a wild kind of polka when Sarah entered, grinning, and said : " There is a man, mum, at the door who wants to know if you

65

c

seized her round the waist, and we were silly
enough to be executing a wild kind of polka
when Sarah entered.

want any good coals." Most annoyed at this. Spent the evening in answering, and tearing up again, the reply to the Mansion House, having left word with Sarah if Gowing or Cummings called we were not at home. Must consult Mr. Perkupp how to answer the Lord Mayor's invitation.

May 1. Carrie said : " I should like to send mother the invitation to look at." I consented, as soon as I had answered it. I told Mr. Perkupp, at the office, with a feeling of pride, that we had received an invitation to the Mansion House ; and he said, to my astonishment, that he himself gave in my name to the Lord Mayor's secretary. I felt this rather discounted the value of the invitation, but I thanked him ; and in reply to me, he described how I was to answer it. I felt the reply was too simple ; but of course Mr. Perkupp knows best.

May 2. Sent my dress-coat and trousers to the little tailor's round the corner, to have the creases taken out. Told Gowing not to call next Monday, as we were going to the Mansion House. Sent similar note to Cummings.

May 3. Carrie went to Mrs. James, at Sutton, to consult about her dress for next Monday. While speaking incidentally to Spotch, one of our head clerks, about the Mansion House, he said : " Oh, I'm asked, but don't think I shall go." When a vulgar man like Spotch is asked I feel my invitation is considerably discounted. In the evening, while I was out, the little tailor brought round my coat and trousers, and because Sarah had not a shilling to pay for the pressing, he took them away again.

May 4. Carrie's mother returned the Lord Mayor's invitation, which was sent to her to look at, with apologies for having upset a glass of port over it. I was too angry to say anything.

May 5. Bought a pair of lavender kid-gloves for next Monday, and two white ties, in case one got spoiled in the tying.

May 6, Sunday. A very dull sermon, during which, I regret to say, I twice thought of the Mansion House reception to-morrow.

May 7. A big red-letter day; viz., the Lord Mayor's reception. The whole house upset. I had to get dressed at half-past six, as Carrie wanted the room to herself. Mrs. James had come up from Sutton to help Carrie; so I could not help thinking it unreasonable that she should require the entire attention of Sarah, the servant, as well. Sarah kept running out of the house to fetch " something for missis," and several times I had, in my full evening-dress, to answer the back-door.

The last time it was the greengrocer's boy, who, not seeing it was me, for Sarah had not lighted the gas, pushed into my hands two cabbages and half-a-dozen coal-blocks. I indignantly threw them on the ground, and felt so annoyed that I so far forgot myself as to box the boy's ears. He went away crying, and said he should summons me, a thing I would not have happen for the world. In the dark, I stepped on a piece of the cabbage, which brought me down on the flags all of a heap. For a moment I was stunned, but when I recovered I crawled upstairs into the drawing-room and on looking into the chimney-glass discovered that my chin was bleeding, my shirt smeared with the coal-blocks, and my left trouser torn at the knee.

However, Mrs. James brought me down another shirt, which I changed in the drawing-room. I put a piece of court-plaster on my chin, and Sarah very neatly sewed up the tear at the knee. At nine o'clock Carrie swept into the room, looking like a queen. Never have I seen her look so lovely, or so distinguished. She was wearing a satin dress of sky-blue—my favourite colour—and a piece of lace, which Mrs. James lent her, round the shoulders, to give a finish. I thought perhaps the dress was a little too long behind, and decidedly too short in front, but Mrs. James said it was *à la mode*. Mrs. James was most kind, and lent Carrie a fan of ivory with red feathers, the value of which, she said, was priceless, as the feathers belonged to the Kachu eagle—a bird now extinct. I preferred the little white fan which Carrie bought for

The greengrocer's boy . . . who pushed into my hands two cabbages and half-a-dozen coal-blocks.

three-and-six at Shoolbred's, but both ladies sat on me at once.

We arrived at the Mansion House too early, which was rather fortunate, for I had an opportunity of speaking to his lordship, who graciously condescended to talk with me some minutes; but I must say I was disappointed to find he did not even know Mr. Perkupp, the principal.

I felt as if we had been invited to the Mansion House by one who did not know the Lord Mayor himself. Crowds arrived, and I shall never forget the grand sight. My humble pen can never describe it. I was a little annoyed with Carrie, who kept saying : " Isn't it a pity we don't know anybody ? "

Once she quite lost her head. I saw someone who looked like Franching, from Peckham, and was moving towards him when she seized me by the coat-tails, and said quite loudly : " Don't leave me," which caused an elderly gentleman, in a court-suit, and a chain round him, and two ladies, to burst out laughing. There was an immense crowd in the supper-room, and, my stars ! it was a splendid supper—any amount of champagne.

Carrie made a most hearty supper, for which I was pleased ; for I sometimes think she is not strong. There was scarcely a dish she did not taste. I was so thirsty, I could not eat much. Receiving a sharp slap on the shoulder, I turned, and, to my amazement, saw Farmerson, our ironmonger. He said, in the most familiar way :

" This is better than Brickfield Terrace, eh ? "
I simply looked at him, and said coolly : " I never
expected to see you here." He said, with a loud,
coarse laugh : " I like that—if *you*, why not *me* ? "
I replied : " Certainly." I wish I could have
thought of something better to say. He said :
" Can I get your good lady anything ? " Carrie
said : " No, I thank you," for which I was pleased.
I said, by way of reproof to him : " You never
sent to-day to paint the bath, as I requested."
Farmerson said : " Pardon me, Mr. Pooter, no
shop when we're in company, please."

Before I could think of a reply, one of the
sheriffs, in full Court costume, slapped Farmerson
on the back and hailed him as an old friend, and
asked him to dine with him at his lodge. I was
astonished. For full five minutes they stood
roaring with laughter, and stood digging each
other in the ribs. They kept telling each other
they didn't look a day older. They began
embracing each other and drinking champagne.

To think that a man who mends our scraper
should know any member of our aristocracy ! I
was just moving with Carrie, when Farmerson
seized me rather roughly by the collar, and
addressing the sheriff, said : " Let me introduce
my neighbour, Pooter." He did not even say
" Mister." The sheriff handed me a glass of
champagne. I felt, after all, it was a great honour
to drink a glass of wine with him, and I told him so.
We stood chatting for some time, and at last I said :
" You must excuse me now if I join Mrs. Pooter."

When I approached her, she said : " Don't let me take you away from friends. I am quite happy standing here alone in a crowd, knowing nobody ! "

As it takes two to make a quarrel, and as it was neither the time nor the place for it, I gave my arm to Carrie, and said : " I hope my darling little wife will dance with me, if only for the sake of saying we had danced at the Mansion House as guests of the Lord Mayor." Finding the dancing after supper was less formal, and knowing how much Carrie used to admire my dancing in the days gone by, I put my arm round her waist and we commenced a waltz.

A most unfortunate accident occurred. I had got on a new pair of boots. Foolishly, I had omitted to take Carrie's advice ; namely, to scratch the soles of them with the points of the scissors or to put a little wet on them. I had scarcely started when, like lightning, my left foot slipped away and I came down, the side of my head striking the floor with such violence that for a second or two I did not know what had happened. I need hardly say that Carrie fell with me with equal violence, breaking the comb in her hair and grazing her elbow.

There was a roar of laughter, which was immediately checked when people found that we had really hurt ourselves. A gentleman assisted Carrie to a seat, and I expressed myself pretty strongly on the danger of having a plain polished floor with no carpet or drugget to prevent people slipping. The gentleman, who said his name was

Darwitts, insisted on escorting Carrie to have a glass of wine, an invitation which I was pleased to allow Carrie to accept.

I followed, and met Farmerson, who immediately said, in his loud voice : " Oh, are you the one who went down ? "

I answered with an indignant look.

With execrable taste, he said : " Look here, old man, we are too old for this game. We must leave these capers to the youngsters. Come and have another glass, that is more in our line."

Although I felt I was buying his silence by accepting, we followed the others into the supper-room.

Neither Carrie nor I, after our unfortunate mishap, felt inclined to stay longer. As we were departing, Farmerson said : " Are you going ; if so, you might give me a lift."

I thought it better to consent, but wish I had first consulted Carrie.

AFTER THE MANSION HOUSE BALL. CARRIE OFFENDED. GOWING ALSO OFFENDED. A PLEASANT PARTY AT THE CUMMINGS'. MR. FRANCHING, OF PECKHAM, VISITS US.

CHAPTER V

May 8. I WOKE up with a most terrible headache. I could scarcely see, and the back of my neck was as if I had given it a crick. I thought first of sending for a doctor; but I did not think it necessary. When up, I felt faint, and went to Brownish's, the chemist, who gave me a draught. So bad at the office, had to get leave to come home. Went to another chemist in the City, and I got a draught. Brownish's dose seems to have made me worse; have eaten nothing all day. To make matters worse, Carrie, every time I spoke to her, answered me sharply—that is, when she answered at all.

In the evening I felt very much worse again and said to her: "I do believe I've been poisoned by the lobster mayonnaise at the Mansion House last night;" she simply replied, without taking her eyes from her sewing: "Champagne never did agree with you." I felt irritated, and said: "What nonsense you talk; I only had a glass and a half, and you know as well as I do —— " Before I could complete the sentence she bounced out of the room. I sat over an hour waiting for her to return; but as she did not, I determined I would go to bed. I discovered Carrie had gone to bed without even saying "good-night"; leaving me to bar the scullery door and feed the cat. I shall certainly speak to her about this in the morning.

Still a little shaky, with black specks.
May 9.   The *Blackfriars Bi - weekly News* contains a long list of the guests at the Mansion House Ball. Disappointed to find our names omitted, though Farmerson's is in plainly enough with M.L.L. after it, whatever that may mean. More than vexed, because we had ordered a dozen copies to send to our friends. Wrote to the *Blackfriars Bi-weekly News*, pointing out their omission.

Carrie had commenced her breakfast when I entered the parlour. I helped myself to a cup of tea, and I said, perfectly calmly and quietly : " Carrie, I wish a little explanation of your conduct last night."

She replied, " Indeed ! and I desire something more than a *little* explanation of your conduct the night before."

I said, coolly : " Really, I don't understand you."

Carrie said sneeringly : " Probably not ; you were scarcely in a condition to understand anything."

I was astounded at this insinuation and simply ejaculated : " Caroline ! "

She said : " Don't be theatrical, it has no effect on me. Reserve that tone for your new friend, *Mister* Farmerson, the ironmonger."

I was about to speak, when Carrie, in a temper such as I have never seen her in before, told me to

hold my tongue. She said : " Now *I'm* going to
say something ! After professing to snub Mr.
Farmerson, you permit him to snub *you*, in my
presence, and then accept his invitation to take a
glass of champagne with you, and you don't limit
yourself to one glass. You then offer this vulgar
man, who made a bungle of repairing our scraper,
a seat in our cab on the way home. I say nothing
about his tearing my dress in getting in the cab,
nor of treading on Mrs. James's expensive fan,
which you knocked out of my hand, and for which
he never even apologised ; but you smoked all the
way home without having the decency to ask my
permission. That is not all ! At the end of the
journey, although he did not offer you a farthing
towards his share of the cab, you asked him in.
Fortunately, he was sober enough to detect, from
my manner, that his company was not desirable."

Goodness knows I felt humiliated enough at
this ; but, to make matters worse, Gowing entered
the room, without knocking, with two hats on his
head and holding the garden-rake in his hand,
with Carrie's fur tippet (which he had taken off
the downstairs hall-peg) round his neck, and
announced himself in a loud, coarse voice : " His
Royal Highness, the Lord Mayor ! " He marched
twice round the room like a buffoon, and finding
we took no notice, said : " Hulloh ! what's up ?
Lovers' quarrel, eh ? "

There was a silence for a moment, so I said
quietly : " My dear Gowing, I'm not very well,
and not quite in the humour for joking ; especially

*Mr. Farmerson smokes all the way home
in the cab.*

when you enter the room without knocking, an act which I fail to see the fun of."

Gowing said : " I'm very sorry, but I called for my stick, which I thought you would have sent round." I handed him his stick, which I remembered I had painted black with the enamel paint, thinking to improve it. He looked at it for a minute with a dazed expression and said : " Who did this ? "

I said : " Eh, did what ? "

He said : " Did what ? Why, destroyed my stick ! It belonged to my poor uncle, and I value it more than anything I have in the world ! I'll know who did it."

I said : " I'm very sorry. I dare say it will come off. I did it for the best."

Gowing said : " Then all I can say is, it's a confounded liberty ; and I *would* add, you're a bigger fool than you look, only *that's* absolutely impossible."

May 12. Got a single copy of the *Blackfriars Bi-weekly News*. There was a short list of several names they had omitted ; but the stupid people had mentioned our names as " Mr. and Mrs. C. Porter." Most annoying ! Wrote again and I took particular care to write our name in capital letters, *POOTER*, so that there should be no possible mistake this time.

May 16. Absolutely disgusted on opening the *Blackfriars Bi-weekly News* of to-day, to find the following paragraph :

" We have received two letters from Mr. and Mrs. Charles Pewter, requesting us to announce the important fact that they were at the Mansion House Ball." I tore up the paper and threw it in the waste-paper basket. My time is far too valuable to bother about such trifles.

May 21.   The last week or ten days terribly dull, Carrie being away at Mrs. James's, at Sutton. Cummings also away. Gowing, I presume, is still offended with me for black-enamelling his stick without asking him.

May 22.   Purchased a new stick mounted with silver, which cost seven-and-sixpence (shall tell Carrie five shillings), and sent it round with nice note to Gowing.

May 23.   Received strange note from Gowing ; he said : " Offended ? not a bit, my boy. I thought you were offended with me for losing my temper. Besides, I found after all it was not my poor old uncle's stick you painted. It was only a shilling thing I bought at a tobacconist's. However, I am much obliged to you for your handsome present all same."

May 24.   Carrie back. Hoorah ! She looks wonderfully well, except that the sun has caught her nose.

May 25. Carrie brought down some of my shirts and advised me to take them to Trillip's round the corner. She said : " The fronts and cuffs are much frayed." I said without a moment's hesitation : " I'm *frayed* they are." Lor! how we roared. I thought we should never stop laughing. As I happened to be sitting next the driver going to town on the 'bus, I told him my joke about the " frayed " shirts. I thought he would have rolled off his seat. They laughed at the office a good bit too over it.

May 26. Left the shirts to be repaired at Trillip's. I said to him : " I'm *'fraid* they are *frayed*." He said, without a smile : " They're bound to do that, sir." Some people seem to be quite destitute of a sense of humour.

June 1. The last week has been like old times, Carrie being back, and Gowing and Cummings calling every evening nearly. Twice we sat out in the garden quite late. This evening we were like a pack of children, and played " consequences." It is a good game.

June 2. " Consequences " again this evening. Not quite so successful as last night ; Gowing having several times over-stepped the limits of good taste.

                    In the evening Carrie and I went
June 4.   round to Mr. and Mrs. Cummings'
                    to spend a quiet evening with them.
Gowing was there, also Mr. Stillbrook. It was
quiet but pleasant. Mrs. Cummings sang five or
six songs, " No, Sir," and " The Garden of Sleep,"
being best in my humble judgment; but what
pleased me most was the duet she sang with Carrie
—classical duet, too. I think it is called, " I would
that my love ! " It was beautiful. If Carrie had
been in better voice, I don't think professionals
could have sung it better. After supper we made
them sing it again. I never liked Mr. Stillbrook
since the walk that Sunday to the " Cow and
Hedge," but I must say he sings comic-songs well.
His song : " We don't want the old men now,"
made us shriek with laughter, especially the verse
referring to Mr. Gladstone ; but there was one
verse I think he might have omitted, and I
said so, but Gowing thought it was the best of
the lot.

                    Trillip brought round the shirts and,
June 6.   to my disgust, his charge for repairing
                    was more than I gave for them when
new. I told him so, and he impertinently replied :
" Well, they are better now than when they were
new." I paid him, and said it was a robbery.
He said : " If you wanted your shirt - fronts
made out of pauper - linen, such as is used for
packing and book-binding, why didn't you say
so ? "

Mr. Franching, of Peckham.

A dreadful annoyance. Met Mr.
June 7. Franching, who lives at Peckham, and
who is a great swell in his way. I
ventured to ask him to come home to meat-tea,
and take pot-luck. I did not think he would
accept such a humble invitation; but he did,
saying, in a most friendly way, he would rather
" peck " with us than by himself. I said : " We
had better get into this blue 'bus." He replied :
" No blue-bussing for me. I have had enough of
the blues lately. I lost a cool ' thou ' over the
Copper Scare. Step in here."

We drove up home in style, in a hansom-cab,
and I knocked three times at the front door
without getting an answer. I saw Carrie, through
the panels of ground-glass (with stars), rushing
upstairs. I told Mr. Franching to wait at the
door while I went round to the side. There I
saw the grocer's boy actually picking off the paint
on the door, which had formed into blisters. No
time to reprove him ; so went round and effected
an entrance through the kitchen window. I let
in Mr. Franching, and showed him into the
drawing-room. I went upstairs to Carrie, who
was changing her dress, and told her I had
persuaded Mr. Franching to come home. She
replied : " How can you do such a thing ? You
know it's Sarah's holiday, and there's not a thing
in the house, the cold mutton having turned with
the hot weather."

Eventually Carrie, like a good creature as she
is, slipped down, washed up the teacups, and laid

*The grocer's boy was actually picking off the paint
on the side door, which had formed into blisters.*

the cloth, and I gave Franching our views of Japan to look at while I ran round to the butcher's to get three chops.

July 30. The miserable cold weather is either upsetting me or Carrie, or both. We seem to break out into an argument about absolutely nothing, and this unpleasant state of things usually occurs at meal-times.

This morning, for some unaccountable reason, we were talking about balloons, and we were as merry as possible ; but the conversation drifted into family matters, during which Carrie, without the slightest reason, referred in the most uncomplimentary manner to my poor father's pecuniary trouble. I retorted by saying that " Pa, at all events, was a gentleman," whereupon Carrie burst out crying. I positively could not eat any breakfast.

At the office I was sent for by Mr. Perkupp, who said he was very sorry, but I should have to take my annual holidays from next Saturday. Franching called at office and asked me to dine at his club, " The Constitutional." Fearing disagreeables at home after the " tiff " this morning, I sent a telegram to Carrie, telling her I was going out to dine and she was not to sit up. Bought a little silver bangle for Carrie.

July 31. Carrie was very pleased with the bangle, which I left with an affectionate note on her dressing-table last night before going to bed. I told

Carrie we should have to start for our holiday next Saturday. She replied quite happily that she did not mind, except that the weather was so bad, and she feared that Miss Jibbons would not be able to get her a seaside dress in time. I told Carrie that I thought the drab one with pink bows looked quite good enough; and Carrie said she should not think of wearing it. I was about to discuss the matter, when, remembering the argument yesterday, resolved to hold my tongue.

I said to Carrie: "I don't think we can do better than 'Good old Broadstairs.'" Carrie not only, to my astonishment, raised an objection to Broadstairs, for the first time, but begged me not to use the expression, "Good old," but to leave it to Mr. Stillbrook and other *gentlemen* of his type. Hearing my 'bus pass the window, I was obliged to rush out of the house without kissing Carrie as usual; and I shouted to her: "I leave it to you to decide." On returning in the evening, Carrie said she thought as the time was so short she had decided on Broadstairs, and had written to Mrs. Beck, Harbour View Terrace, for apartments.

August 1.   Ordered a new pair of trousers at Edwards's, and told them not to cut them so loose over the boot; the last pair being so loose and also tight at the knee, looked like a sailor's, and I heard Pitt, that objectionable youth at the office, call out "Hornpipe"

*Young Pitt called out " Hornpipe " as I passed
his desk.*

as I passed his desk. Carrie has ordered of Miss Jibbons a pink Garibaldi and blue-serge skirt, which I always think looks so pretty at the seaside. In the evening she trimmed herself a little sailor-hat, while I read to her the *Exchange and Mart*. We had a good laugh over my trying on the hat when she had finished it; Carrie saying it looked so funny with my beard, and how the people would have roared if I went on the stage like it.

August 2. Mrs. Beck wrote to say we could have our usual rooms at Broadstairs. That's off our mind. Bought a coloured shirt and a pair of tan-coloured boots, which I see many of the swell clerks wearing in the City, and hear are all the " go."

August 3. A beautiful day. Looking forward to to-morrow. Carrie bought a parasol about five feet long. I told her it was ridiculous. She said : " Mrs. James, of Sutton, has one twice as long ; " so the matter dropped. I bought a capital hat for hot weather at the seaside. I don't know what it is called, but it is the shape of the helmet worn in India, only made of straw. Got three new ties, two coloured handkerchiefs, and a pair of navy-blue socks at Pope Brothers. Spent the evening packing. Carrie told me not to forget to borrow Mr. Higgsworth's telescope, which he always lends me, knowing I know how to take care of it.

Sent Sarah out for it. While everything was
seeming so bright, the last post brought us a letter
from Mrs. Beck, saying : " I have just let all my
house to one party, and am sorry I must take
back my words, and am sorry you must find other
apartments ; but Mrs. Womming, next door, will
be pleased to accommodate you, but she cannot
take you before Monday, as her rooms are engaged
Bank Holiday week."

THE UNEXPECTED ARRIVAL
HOME OF OUR SON,
WILLIE LUPIN POOTER.

CHAPTER VI

August 4. THE first post brought a nice letter from our dear son Willie, acknowledging a trifling present which Carrie sent him, the day before yesterday being his twentieth birthday. To our utter amazement he turned up himself in the afternoon, having journeyed all the way from Oldham. He said he had got leave from the bank, and as Monday was a holiday he thought he would give us a little surprise.

August 5, Sunday. We have not seen Willie since last Christmas, and are pleased to notice what a fine young man he has grown. One would scarcely believe he was Carrie's son. He looks more like a younger brother. I rather disapprove of his wearing a check suit on a Sunday, and I think he ought to have gone to church this morning ; but he said he was tired after yesterday's journey, so I refrained from any remark on the subject. We had a bottle of port for dinner, and drank dear Willie's health. He said : " Oh, by-the-by, did I tell you I've cut my first name, ' William,' and taken the second name ' Lupin ' ? In fact, I'm only known at Oldham as ' Lupin Pooter.' If you were to

' Willie' me there, they wouldn't know what you meant."

Of course, Lupin being a purely family name, Carrie was delighted, and began by giving a long history of the Lupins. I ventured to say that I thought William a nice simple name, and reminded him he was christened after his Uncle William, who was much respected in the City. Willie, in a manner which I did not much care for, said sneeringly : " Oh, I know all about that—Good old Bill ! " and helped himself to a third glass of port.

Carrie objected strongly to my saying " Good old," but she made no remark when Willie used the double adjective. I said nothing, but looked at her, which meant more. I said : " My dear Willie, I hope you are happy with your colleagues at the Bank." He replied : " Lupin, if you please ; and with respect to the Bank, there's not a clerk who is a gentleman, and the ' boss ' is a cad." I felt so shocked, I could say nothing, and my instinct told me there was something wrong.

August 6, *Bank Holiday.* As there was no sign of Lupin moving at nine o'clock, I knocked at his door, and said we usually breakfasted at half-past eight, and asked how long would he be ? Lupin replied that he had had a lively time of it, first with the train shaking the house all night, and then with the sun streaming in through the window in his eyes, and

Lupin.

giving him a cracking headache. Carrie came up and asked if he would like some breakfast sent up, and he said he could do with a cup of tea, and didn't want anything to eat.

Lupin not having come down, I went up again at half-past one, and said we dined at two; he said he "would be there." He never came down till a quarter to three. I said: "We have not seen much of you, and you will have to return by the 5.30 train; therefore you will have to leave in an hour, unless you go by the midnight mail." He said: "Look here, Guv'nor, it's no use beating about the bush. I've tendered my resignation at the Bank."

For a moment I could not speak. When my speech came again, I said: "How dare you, sir? How dare you take such a serious step without consulting me? Don't answer me, sir!—you will sit down immediately, and write a note at my dictation, withdrawing your resignation and amply apologising for your thoughtlessness."

Imagine my dismay when he replied with a loud guffaw: "It's no use. If you want the good old truth, I've got the chuck!"

August 7.   Mr. Perkupp has given me leave to postpone my holiday a week, as we could not get the room. This will give us an opportunity of trying to find an appointment for Willie before we go. The ambition of my life would be to get him into Mr. Perkupp's firm.

August 11.
Although it is a serious matter having our boy Lupin on our hands, still it is satisfactory to know he was asked to resign from the Bank simply because "he took no interest in his work, and always arrived an hour (sometimes two hours) late." We can all start off on Monday to Broadstairs with a light heart. This will take my mind off the worry of the last few days, which have been wasted over a useless correspondence with the manager of the Bank at Oldham.

August 13.
Hurrah! at Broadstairs. Very nice apartments near the station. On the cliffs they would have been double the price. The landlady had a nice five o'clock dinner and tea ready, which we all enjoyed, though Lupin seemed fastidious because there happened to be a fly in the butter. It was very wet in the evening, for which I was thankful, as it was a good excuse for going to bed early. Lupin said he would sit up and read a bit.

August 14.
I was a little annoyed to find Lupin, instead of reading last night, had gone to a common sort of entertainment, given at the Assembly Rooms. I expressed my opinion that such performances were unworthy of respectable patronage ; but he replied : " Oh, it was only 'for one night only.' I had a fit of the blues come on, and thought I would go to see Polly Presswell, England's Particular Spark." I

told him I was proud to say I had never heard of her. Carrie said : " Do let the boy alone. He's quite old enough to take care of himself, and won't forget he's a gentleman. Remember, you were young once yourself." Rained all day hard, but Lupin would go out.

August 15. Cleared up a bit, so we all took the train to Margate, and the first person we met on the jetty was Gowing. I said : " Hulloh ! I thought you had gone to Barmouth with your Birmingham friends ? " He said : " Yes, but young Peter Lawrence was so ill, they postponed their visit, so I came down here. You know the Cummings' are here too ? " Carrie said : " Oh, that will be delightful ! We must have some evenings together and have games."

I introduced Lupin, saying : " You will be pleased to find we have our dear boy at home ! " Gowing said : " How's that ? You don't mean to say he's left the Bank ? "

I changed the subject quickly, and thereby avoided any of those awkward questions which Gowing always has a knack of asking.

August 16. Lupin positively refused to walk down the Parade with me because I was wearing my new straw helmet with my frock-coat. I don't know what the boy is coming to.

*Lupin positively refused to walk down the
Parade with me because I was wearing my
new straw helmet with my frock-coat.*

August 17.   Lupin not falling in with our views, Carrie and I went for a sail. It was a relief to be with her alone ; for when Lupin irritates me, she always sides with him. On our return, he said : " Oh, you've been on the ' Shilling Emetic,' have you ? You'll come to six-pennorth on the ' Liver Jerker ' next." I presume he meant a tricycle, but I affected not to understand him.

August 18.   Gowing and Cummings walked over to arrange an evening at Margate. It being wet, Gowing asked Cummings to accompany him to the hotel and have a game of billiards, knowing I never play, and in fact disapprove of the game. Cummings said he must hasten back to Margate ; whereupon Lupin, to my horror, said : " I'll give you a game, Gowing—a hundred up. A walk round the cloth will give me an appetite for dinner." I said : " Perhaps *Mister* Gowing does not care to play with boys." Gowing surprised me by saying : " Oh yes, I do, if they play well," and they walked off together.

August 19, *Sunday*.   I was about to read Lupin a sermon on smoking (which he indulges in violently) and billiards, but he put on his hat and walked out. Carrie then read *me* a long sermon on the palpable inadvisability of treating Lupin as if he were a mere child. I felt she was somewhat right, so in

the evening I offered him a cigar. He seemed
pleased, but, after a few whiffs, said : " This is a
good old tup'ny—try one of mine," and he handed
me a cigar as long as it was strong, which is saying
a good deal.

August 20. I am glad our last day at the seaside
was fine, though clouded overhead.
We went over to Cummings' (at
Margate) in the evening, and as it was cold, we
stayed in and played games ; Gowing, as usual,
overstepping the mark. He suggested we should
play " Cutlets," a game we never heard of. He
sat on a chair, and asked Carrie to sit on his lap,
an invitation which dear Carrie rightly declined.

After some species of wrangling, *I* sat on
Gowing's knees and Carrie sat on the edge of
mine. Lupin sat on the edge of Carrie's lap, then
Cummings on Lupin's and Mrs. Cummings on
her husband's. We looked very ridiculous, and
laughed a good deal.

Gowing then said : " Are you a believer in the
Great Mogul ? " We had to answer all together :
" Yes—oh, yes ! " (three times). Gowing said :
" So am I," and suddenly got up. The result of
this stupid joke was that we all fell on the ground,
and poor Carrie banged her head against the
corner of the fender. Mrs. Cummings put some
vinegar on ; but through this we missed the last
train, and had to drive back to Broadstairs, which
cost me seven-and-sixpence.

W. C.

We play the game of "Cutlets." When we had all sat on each other's laps, Gowing said : "Are you a believer in the Great Mogul?"

Gowing said : "So am I," and suddenly got up.

HOME AGAIN.   MRS. JAMES'S INFLUENCE
ON CARRIE.   CAN GET NOTHING FOR
LUPIN.   NEXT-DOOR NEIGHBOURS AR⁻ A
LITTLE TROUBLESOME. SOMEONE TAMPERS
WITH MY DIARY.   GOT A PLACE FOR
LUPIN.   LUPIN STARTLES US WITH AN
ANNOUNCEMENT.

CHAPTER VII

HOME, sweet Home again ! Carrie
August 22. bought some pretty blue-wool mats
to stand vases on. Fripps, Janus
and Co. write to say they are sorry they have no
vacancy among their staff of clerks for Lupin.

I bought a pair of stags' heads made
August 23. of plaster - of - Paris and coloured
brown. They will look just the thing
for our little hall, and give it style ; the heads are
excellent imitations. Poolers and Smith are sorry
they have nothing to offer Lupin.

Simply to please Lupin, and make
August 24. things cheerful for him, as he is a
little down, Carrie invited Mrs.
James to come up from Sutton and spend two or
three days with us. We have not said a word to
Lupin, but mean to keep it as a surprise.

Mrs. James, of Sutton, arrived in
August 25. the afternoon, bringing with her an
enormous bunch of wild flowers.
The more I see of Mrs. James the nicer I think
she is, and she is devoted to Carrie. She went
into Carrie's room to take off her bonnet, and
remained there nearly an hour talking about dress.

I hung up a stag's head made of plaster-of-Paris.

Lupin said he was not a bit surprised at Mrs. James's *visit*, but was surprised at *her*.

August 26, Sunday.   Nearly late for church, Mrs. James having talked considerably about what to wear all the morning. Lupin does not seem to get on very well with Mrs. James. I am afraid we shall have some trouble with our next-door neighbours who came in last Wednesday. Several of their friends, who drive up in dog-carts, have already made themselves objectionable.

An evening or two ago I had put on a white waistcoat for coolness, and while walking past with my thumbs in my waistcoat pockets (a habit I have), one man, seated in the cart, and looking like an American, commenced singing some vulgar nonsense about "*I had thirteen dollars in my waistcoat pocket.*" I fancied it was meant for me, and my suspicions were confirmed; for while walking round the garden in my tall hat this afternoon a "throw-down" cracker was deliberately aimed at my hat, and exploded on it like a percussion cap. I turned sharply, and am positive I saw the man who was in the cart retreating from one of the bedroom windows.

August 27.   Carrie and Mrs. James went off shopping, and had not returned when I came back from the office. Judging from the subsequent conversation, I am afraid Mrs. James is filling Carrie's head with a lot of nonsense about dress. I walked over to Gowing's and asked him to drop in to supper, and make things pleasant.

Carrie prepared a little extemporised supper, consisting of the remainder of the cold joint, a small piece of salmon (which I was to refuse, in case there was not enough to go round), and a blanc-mange and custards. There was also a decanter of port and some jam puffs on the sideboard. Mrs. James made us play rather a good game of cards, called "Muggins." To my surprise, in fact disgust, Lupin got up in the middle, and, in a most sarcastic tone, said : " Pardon me, this sort of thing is too fast for me. I shall go and enjoy a quiet game of marbles in the back-garden."

Things might have become rather disagreeable but for Gowing (who seems to have taken to Lupin) suggesting they should invent games. Lupin said : " Let's play ' monkeys.' " He then led Gowing all round the room, and brought him in front of the looking-glass. I must confess I laughed heartily at this. I was a little vexed at everybody subsequently laughing at some joke which they did not explain, and it was only on going to bed I discovered I must have been walking about all the evening with an antimacassar on one button of my coat-tails.

August 28. Found a large brick in the middle bed of geraniums, evidently come from next door. Pattles and Pattles can't find a place for Lupin.

August 29. Mrs. James is making a positive fool of Carrie. Carrie appeared in a new dress like a smock-frock. She said " smocking " was all the rage. I replied it put me in a rage. She also had on a hat as big as a kitchen coal-scuttle, and the same shape. Mrs. James went home, and both Lupin and I were somewhat pleased — the first time we have agreed on a single subject since his return. Merkins and Son write they have no vacancy for Lupin.

October 30. I should very much like to know who has wilfully torn the last five or six weeks out of my diary. It is perfectly monstrous! Mine is a large scribbling diary, with plenty of space for the record of my everyday events, and in keeping up that record I take (with much pride) a great deal of pains.

I asked Carrie if she knew anything about it. She replied it was my own fault for leaving the diary about with a charwoman cleaning and the sweeps in the house. I said that was not an answer to my question. This retort of mine, which I thought extremely smart, would have been more effective had I not jogged my elbow against a vase on a table temporarily placed in the passage, knocked it over, and smashed it.

Carrie was dreadfully upset at this disaster, for it was one of a pair of vases which cannot be matched, given to us on our wedding-day by

Mrs. Burtsett, an old friend of Carrie's cousins, the Pommertons, late of Dalston. I called to Sarah, and asked her about the diary. She said she had not been in the sitting-room at all; after the sweep had left, Mrs. Birrell (the charwoman) had cleaned the room and lighted the fire herself. Finding a burnt piece of paper in the grate, I examined it, and found it was a piece of my diary. So it was evident someone had torn my diary to light the fire. I requested Mrs. Birrell to be sent to me to-morrow.

October 31. Received a letter from our principal, Mr. Perkupp, saying that he thinks he knows of a place at last for our dear boy Lupin. This, in a measure, consoles me for the loss of a portion of my diary; for I am bound to confess the last few weeks have been devoted to the record of disappointing answers received from people to whom I have applied for appointments for Lupin. Mrs. Birrell called, and, in reply to me, said: "She never *see* no book, much less take such a liberty as *touch* it."

I said I was determined to find out who did it, whereupon she said she would do her best to help me; but she remembered the sweep lighting the fire with a bit of the *Echo*. I requested the sweep to be sent to me to-morrow. I wish Carrie had not given Lupin a latch-key; we never seem to see anything of him. I sat up till past one for him, and then retired tired.

Mr. Perkupp

November 1.

My entry yesterday about "retired tired," which I did not notice at the time, is rather funny. If I were not so worried just now, I might have had a little joke about it. The sweep called, but had the audacity to come up to the hall-door and lean his dirty bag of soot on the door-step. He, however, was so polite, I could not rebuke him. He said Sarah lighted the fire. Unfortunately, Sarah heard this, for she was dusting the banisters, and she ran down, and flew into a temper with the sweep, causing a row on the front door-steps, which I would not have had happen for anything. I ordered her about her business, and told the sweep I was sorry to have troubled him ; and so I was, for the door-steps were covered with soot in consequence of his visit. I would willingly give ten shillings to find out who tore my diary.

November 2.

I spent the evening quietly with Carrie, of whose company I never tire. We had a most pleasant chat about the letters on " Is Marriage a Failure ? " It has been no failure in our case. In talking over our own happy experiences, we never noticed that it was past midnight. We were startled by hearing the door slam violently. Lupin had come in. He made no attempt to turn down the gas in the passage, or even to look into the room where we were, but went straight up to bed, making a terrible noise. I asked him to come down for a moment, and he begged to be excused,

Lupin said: "I'm engaged to be married."

as he was " dead beat," an observation that was
scarcely consistent with the fact that, for a quarter
of an hour afterwards, he was positively dancing
in his room, and shouting out, " See me dance
the polka ! " or some such nonsense.

November 3. Good news at last. Mr. Perkupp
has got an appointment for Lupin,
and he is to go and see about it on
Monday. Oh, how my mind is relieved ! I went
to Lupin's room to take the good news to him,
but he was in bed, very seedy, so I resolved to
keep it over till the evening.

He said he had last night been elected a member
of an Amateur Dramatic Club, called the
" Holloway Comedians " ; and, though it was a
pleasant evening, he had sat in a draught, and got
neuralgia in the head. He declined to have any
breakfast, so I left him.

In the evening I had up a special bottle of port,
and, Lupin being in for a wonder, we filled our
glasses, and I said : " Lupin my boy, I have some
good and unexpected news for you. Mr. Perkupp
has procured you an appointment ! " Lupin said :
" Good biz ! " and we drained our glasses.

Lupin then said : " Fill up the glasses again, for
I have some good and unexpected news for you."

I had some slight misgivings, and so evidently
had Carrie, for she said : " I hope we shall think
it good news."

Lupin said : " Oh, it's all right ! *I'm engaged
to be married !* "

CHAPTER VIII

CARRIE and I troubled about that mere boy Lupin getting engaged to be married without consulting us or anything. After dinner he told us all about it. He said the lady's name was Daisy Mutlar, and she was the nicest, prettiest, and most accomplished girl he ever met. He loved her the moment he saw her, and if he had to wait fifty years he would wait, and he knew she would wait for him.

November 5, Sunday.

Lupin further said, with much warmth, that the world was a different world to him now,—it was a world worth living in. He lived with an object now, and that was to make Daisy Mutlar—Daisy Pooter, and he would guarantee she would not disgrace the family of the Pooters. Carrie here burst out crying, and threw her arms round his neck, and in doing so upset the glass of port he held in his hand all over his new light trousers.

I said I had no doubt we should like Miss Mutlar when we saw her, but Carrie said she loved her already. I thought this rather premature, but held my tongue. Daisy Mutlar was the sole topic of conversation for the remainder of the day. I asked Lupin who her people were, and he replied : " Oh, you know Mutlar, Williams and Watts." I did not know, but refrained from asking any further questions at present, for fear of irritating Lupin.

November 6. Lupin went with me to the office, and had a long conversation with Mr. Perkupp, our principal, the result of which was that he accepted a clerkship in the firm of Job Cleanands and Co., Stock and Share Brokers. Lupin told me, privately, it was an advertising firm, and he did not think much of it. I replied : " Beggars should not be choosers ; " and I will do Lupin the justice to say, he looked rather ashamed of himself.

In the evening we went round to the Cummings', to have a few fireworks. It began to rain, and I thought it rather dull. One of my squibs would not go off, and Gowing said : " Hit it on your boot, boy ; it will go off then." I gave it a few knocks on the end of my boot, and it went off with one loud explosion, and burnt my fingers rather badly. I gave the rest of the squibs to the little Cummings' boy to let off.

Another unfortunate thing happened, which brought a heap of abuse on my head. Cummings fastened a large wheel set-piece on a stake in the ground by way of a grand finale. He made a great fuss about it ; said it cost seven shillings. There was a little difficulty in getting it alight. At last it went off ; but after a couple of slow revolutions it stopped. I had my stick with me, so I gave it a tap to send it round, and, unfortunately, it fell off the stake on to the grass. Anybody would have thought I had set the house on fire from the way in which they stormed at me. I will never join in any more firework parties. It is a ridiculous waste of time and money.

November 7. Lupin asked Carrie to call on Mrs. Mutlar, but Carrie said she thought Mrs. Mutlar ought to call on her first. I agreed with Carrie, and this led to an argument. However, the matter was settled by Carrie saying she could not find any visiting cards, and we must get some more printed, and when they were finished would be quite time enough to discuss the etiquette of calling.

November 8. I ordered some of our cards at Black's, the stationer's. I ordered twenty-five of each, which will last us for a good long time. In the evening, Lupin brought in Harry Mutlar, Miss Mutlar's brother. He was rather a gawky youth, and Lupin said he was the most popular and best amateur in the club, referring to the "Holloway Comedians." Lupin whispered to us that if we could only "draw out" Harry a bit, he would make us roar with laughter.

At supper, young Mutlar did several amusing things. He took up a knife, and with the flat part of it played a tune on his cheek in a wonderful manner. He also gave an imitation of an old man with no teeth, smoking a big cigar. The way he kept dropping the cigar sent Carrie into fits.

In the course of conversation, Daisy's name cropped up, and young Mutlar said he would bring his sister round to us one evening—his parents being rather old-fashioned, and not going out much. Carrie said we would get up a little special party. As young Mutlar showed no inclination to go, and it was approaching eleven o'clock, as a hint I reminded Lupin that he had to be up early to-morrow. Instead of taking the hint, Mutlar began a series of comic imitations. He went on for an hour without cessation. Poor Carrie could scarcely keep her eyes open. At last she made an excuse, and said " Good-night."

Mutlar then left, and I heard him and Lupin whispering in the hall something about the " Holloway Comedians," and to my disgust, although it was past midnight, Lupin put on his hat and coat, and went out with his new companion.

November 9. My endeavours to discover who tore the sheets out of my diary still fruitless. Lupin has Daisy Mutlar on the brain, so we see little of him, except that he invariably turns up at meal times. Cummings dropped in.

November 10. Lupin seems to like his new berth —that's a comfort. Daisy Mutlar the sole topic of conversation during tea. Carrie almost as full of it as Lupin. Lupin informs me, to my disgust, that he has been persuaded to take part in the forthcoming performance of the " Holloway Comedians." He says he is to play Bob Britches in the farce, *Gone to my Uncle's* ; Frank Mutlar is going to play old Musty. I told Lupin pretty plainly I was not in the least degree interested in the matter, and totally disapproved of amateur theatricals. Gowing came in the evening.

November 11. Returned home to find the house in a most disgraceful uproar. Carrie, who appeared very frightened, was standing outside her bedroom, while Sarah was excited and crying. Mrs. Birrell (the charwoman), who had evidently been drinking, was shouting at the top of her voice that she was " no thief, that she was a respectable woman, who had to work hard for her living, and she would smack anyone's face who put lies into her mouth." Lupin, whose back was towards me, did not hear me come in. He was standing between the two women, and, I regret to say, in his endeavour to act as peacemaker, he made use of rather strong language in the presence of his mother ; and I was just in time to hear him say : " And all this fuss about the loss of a few pages from a rotten diary that wouldn't fetch three-halfpence a pound ! " I said, quietly : " Pardon me, Lupin, that is a matter of opinion ; and as I am master of this house, perhaps you will allow me to take the reins."

I ascertained that the cause of the row was, that Sarah had accused Mrs. Birrell of tearing the pages out of my diary to wrap up some kitchen fat and leavings which she had taken out of the house last week. Mrs. Birrell had slapped Sarah's face, and said she had taken nothing out of the place, as there was "never no leavings to take." I ordered Sarah back to her work, and requested Mrs. Birrell to go home. When I entered the parlour Lupin was kicking his legs in the air, and roaring with laughter.

November 12, *Sunday*. Coming home from church Carrie and I met Lupin, Daisy Mutlar, and her brother. Daisy was introduced to us, and we walked home together, Carrie walking on with Miss Mutlar. We asked them in for a few minutes, and I had a good look at my future daughter-in-law. My heart quite sank. She is a big young woman, and I should think at least eight years older than Lupin. I did not even think her good-looking. Carrie asked her if she could come in on Wednesday next with her brother to meet a few friends. She replied that she would only be too pleased.

November 13. Carrie sent out invitations to Gowing, the Cummings, to Mr. and Mrs. James (of Sutton), and Mr. Stillbrook. I wrote a note to Mr. Franching, of Peckham. Carrie said we may as well make it a nice affair, and why not ask our principal,

Daisy Mutlar.

Mr. Perkupp ? I said I feared we were not quite grand enough for him. Carrie said there was " no offence in asking him." I said : " Certainly not," and I wrote him a letter. Carrie confessed she was a little disappointed with Daisy Mutlar's appearance, but thought she seemed a nice girl.

November 14. Everybody so far has accepted for our quite grand little party for to-morrow. Mr. Perkupp, in a nice letter which I shall keep, wrote that he was dining in Kensington, but if he could get away, he would come up to Holloway for an hour. Carrie was busy all day, making little cakes and open jam puffs and jellies. She said she felt quite nervous about her responsibilities to-morrow evening. We decided to have some light things on the table, such as sandwiches, cold chicken and ham, and some sweets, and on the sideboard a nice piece of cold beef and a Paysandu tongue for the more hungry ones to peg into if they liked.

Gowing called to know if he was to put on " swallow-tails " to-morrow. Carrie said he had better dress, especially as Mr. Franching was coming, and there was a possibility of Mr. Perkupp also putting in an appearance.

Gowing said : " Oh, I only wanted to know ; for I have not worn my dress-coat for some time, and I must send it to have the creases pressed out."

After Gowing left, Lupin came in, and in his

anxiety to please Daisy Mutlar, carped at and criticised the arrangements, and, in fact, disapproved of everything, including our having asked our old friend Cummings, who, he said, would look in evening-dress like a green-grocer engaged to wait, and who must not be surprised if Daisy took him for one.

I fairly lost my temper, and said : " Lupin, allow me to tell you Miss Daisy Mutlar is not the Queen of England. I gave you credit for more wisdom than to allow yourself to be inveigled into an engagement with a woman considerably older than yourself. I advise you to think of earning your living before entangling yourself with a wife whom you will have to support, and, in all probability, her brother also, who appeared to be nothing but a loafer."

Instead of receiving this advice in a sensible manner, Lupin jumped up and said : " If you insult the lady I am engaged to, you insult me. I will leave the house and never darken your doors again."

He went out of the house, slamming the hall-door. But it was all right. He came back to supper, and we played Bézique till nearly twelve o'clock.

OUR FIRST IMPORTANT PARTY. OLD
FRIENDS AND NEW FRIENDS. GOWING
IS A LITTLE ANNOYING ; BUT HIS FRIEND,
MR. STILLBROOK, TURNS OUT TO BE QUITE
AMUSING. INOPPORTUNE ARRIVAL OF
MR. PERKUPP, BUT HE IS MOST KIND AND
COMPLIMENTARY. PARTY A GREAT
SUCCESS.

CHAPTER IX

A RED - LETTER DAY. Our first
November 15. important party since we have been
in this house. I got home early
from the City. Lupin insisted on having a hired
waiter, and stood a half-dozen of champagne. I
think this an unnecessary expense, but Lupin
said he had had a piece of luck, having made
three pounds out of a private deal in the City.
I hope he won't gamble in his new situation.
The supper-room looked so nice, and Carrie
truly said : " We need not be ashamed of its
being seen by Mr. Perkupp, should he honour
us by coming."

I dressed early in case people should arrive
punctually at eight o'clock, and was much vexed
to find my new dress-trousers much too short.
Lupin, who is getting beyond his position, found
fault with my wearing ordinary boots instead of
dress-boots.

I replied satirically : " My dear son, I have
lived to be above that sort of thing."

Lupin burst out laughing, and said : " A
man generally was above his boots."

This may be funny, or it may *not ;* but I was
gratified to find he had not discovered the coral
had come off one of my studs. Carrie looked a
picture, wearing the dress she wore at the Mansion

House. The arrangement of the drawing-room was excellent. Carrie had hung muslin curtains over the folding-doors, and also over one of the entrances, for we had removed the door from its hinges.

Mr. Peters, the waiter, arrived in good time, and I gave him strict orders not to open another bottle of champagne until the previous one was empty. Carrie arranged for some sherry and port wine to be placed on the drawing-room sideboard, with some glasses. By-the-by, our new enlarged and tinted photographs look very nice on the walls, especially as Carrie has arranged some Liberty silk bows on the four corners of them.

The first arrival was Gowing, who, with his usual taste, greeted me with : "Hulloh, Pooter, why your trousers are too short ! "

I simply said : "Very likely, and you will find my temper ' *short* ' also."

He said : " That won't make your trousers longer, Juggins. You should get your missus to put a flounce on them."

I wonder I waste my time entering his insulting observations in my diary.

The next arrivals were Mr. and Mrs. Cummings. The former said : " As you didn't say anything about dress, I have come ' half-dress.' " He had on a black frock-coat and white tie. The James', Mr. Merton, and Mr. Stillbrook arrived, but Lupin was restless and unbearable till his Daisy Mutlar and Frank arrived.

Carrie and I were rather startled at Daisy's

appearance. She had a bright-crimson dress on, cut very low in the neck. I do not think such a style modest. She ought to have taken a lesson from Carrie, and covered her shoulders with a little lace. Mr. Nackles, Mr. Sprice-Hogg and his four daughters came ; so did Franching, and one or two of Lupin's new friends, members of the " Holloway Comedians." Some of these seemed rather theatrical in their manner, especially one, who was posing all the evening, and leant on our little round table and cracked it. Lupin called him " our Henry," and said he was " our lead at the H.C.'s," and was quite as good in that department as Harry Mutlar was as the low-comedy merchant. All this is Greek to me.

We had some music, and Lupin, who never left Daisy's side for a moment, raved over her singing of a song, called " Some Day." It seemed a pretty song, but she made such grimaces, and sang, to my mind, so out of tune, I would not have asked her to sing again ; but Lupin made her sing four songs right off, one after the other.

At ten o'clock we went down to supper, and from the way Gowing and Cummings ate you would have thought they had not had a meal for a month. I told Carrie to keep something back in case Mr. Perkupp should come by mere chance. Gowing annoyed me very much by filling a large tumbler of champagne, and drinking it straight off. He repeated this action, and made me fear our half-dozen of champagne would not last out. I tried to keep a bottle back, but Lupin got hold of it, and took it to the side-table with Daisy and Frank Mutlar.

We went upstairs, and the young fellows began skylarking. Carrie put a stop to that at once. Stillbrook amused us with a song, " What have you done with your Cousin John ? " I did not notice that Lupin and Frank had disappeared. I asked Mr. Watson, one of the Holloways, where they were, and he said : " It's a case of ' Oh, what a surprise ! ' "

We were directed to form a circle—which we did. Watson then said : " I have much pleasure in introducing the celebrated Blondin Donkey." Frank and Lupin then bounded into the room. Lupin had whitened his face like a clown, and Frank had tied round his waist a large hearthrug. He was supposed to be the donkey, and he looked it. They indulged in a very noisy pantomime, and we were all shrieking with laughter.

I turned round suddenly, and then I saw Mr. Perkupp standing half-way in the door, he having arrived without our knowing it. I beckoned to Carrie, and we went up to him at once. He would not come right into the room. I apologised for the foolery, but Mr. Perkupp said : " Oh, it seems amusing." I could see he was not a bit amused.

Carrie and I took him downstairs, but the table was a wreck. There was not a glass of champagne left—not even a sandwich. Mr. Perkupp said he required nothing, but would like a glass of seltzer or soda water. The last syphon was empty. Carrie said: "We have plenty of port wine left." Mr. Perkupp said with a smile: "No, thank you. I really require nothing, but I am most pleased to see you and your husband in your own home. Good-night, Mrs. Pooter—you will excuse my very short stay, I know." I went with him to his carriage, and he said: "Don't trouble to come to the office till twelve to-morrow."

I felt despondent as I went back to the house, and I told Carrie I thought the party was a failure. Carrie said it was a great success, and I was only tired, and insisted on my having some port myself. I drank two glasses, and felt much better, and we went into the drawing-room, where they had commenced dancing. Carrie and I had a little dance, which I said reminded me of old days. She said I was a spooney old thing.

REFLECTIONS. I MAKE ANOTHER GOOD
JOKE. AM ANNOYED AT THE CONSTANT
SERVING-UP OF THE " BLANC-MANGE."
LUPIN EXPRESSES HIS OPINION OF
WEDDINGS. LUPIN FALLS OUT WITH
DAISY MUTLAR.

CHAPTER X

November 16.WOKE about twenty times during the night, with terrible thirst. Finished off all the water in the bottle, as well as half that in the jug. Kept dreaming also, that last night's party was a failure, and that a lot of low people came without invitation. and kept chaffing and throwing things at Mr. Perkupp, till at last I was obliged to hide him in the box-room (which we had just discovered), with a bath-towel over him. It seems absurd now, but it was painfully real in the dream. I had the same dream about a dozen times.

Carrie annoyed me by saying: "You know champagne never agrees with you." I told her I had only a couple of glasses of it, having kept myself entirely to port. I added that good champagne hurt nobody, and Lupin told me he had only got it from a traveller as a favour, as that particular brand had been entirely bought up by a West-End club.

I think I ate too heartily of the "side dishes," as the waiter called them. I said to Carrie: "I wish I had put those 'side dishes' *aside*." I repeated this, but Carrie was busy, packing up the teaspoons we had borrowed of Mrs. Cummings for the party. It was just half-past eleven, and I was starting for the office, when Lupin appeared, with a yellow complexion, and said : " Hulloh ! Guv., what priced head have you this morning ? " I told him he might just as well speak to me in Dutch.   He added : " When I woke this morning, my head was as big as Baldwin's balloon."   On the spur of the moment I said the cleverest thing I think I have ever said ; viz. : " Perhaps that accounts for the para*shooting* pains." We all three roared.

November 17.   Still feel tired and headachy ! In the evening Gowing called, and was full of praise about our party last Wednesday.   He said everything was done beautifully, and he enjoyed himself enormously. Gowing can be a very nice fellow when he likes, but you never know how long it will last.   For instance, he stopped to supper, and seeing some *blanc-mange* on the table, shouted out, while the servant was in the room : " Hulloh ! The remains of Wednesday ? "

November 18.   Woke up quite fresh after a good night's rest, and feel quite myself again.   I am satisfied a life of going-out and Society is not a life for me ; we therefore declined the invitation which we received this morning to Miss Bird's wedding.   We only met her twice at Mrs. James', and it means a present.   Lupin said : " I am with you for once. To my mind a wedding's a very poor play.   There are only two parts in it—the bride and bridegroom.

The best man is only a walking gentleman. With the exception of a crying father and a snivelling mother, the rest are *supers* who have to dress well and have to *pay* for their insignificant parts in the shape of costly presents." I did not care for the theatrical slang, but thought it clever, though disrespectful.

I told Sarah not to bring up the *blanc-mange* again for breakfast. It seems to have been placed on our table at every meal since Wednesday. Cummings came round in the evening, and congratulated us on the success of our party. He said it was the best party he had been to for many a year ; but he wished we had let him know it was full dress, as he would have turned up in his swallow-tails. We sat down to a quiet game of dominoes, and were interrupted by the noisy entrance of Lupin and Frank Mutlar. Cummings and I asked them to join us. Lupin said he did not care for dominoes, and suggested a game of " Spoof." On my asking if it required counters, Frank and Lupin in measured time said : " One, two, three ; go ! Have you an estate in Greenland ? " It was simply Greek to me, but it appears it is one of the customs of the " Holloway Comedians " to do this when a member displays ignorance.

In spite of my instructions, that *blanc-mange* was brought up again for supper. To make matters worse, there had been an attempt to disguise it, by placing it in a glass dish with jam round it. Carrie asked Lupin if he would have some, and he replied : " No second-hand goods for me, thank you." I told Carrie, when we were alone, if that *blanc-mange* were placed on the table again I should walk out of the house.

A delightfully quiet day. In the afternoon Lupin was off to spend the rest of the day with the Mutlars.

November 19,
Sunday.

He departed in the best of spirits, and Carrie said : " Well, one advantage of Lupin's engagement with Daisy is that the boy seems happy all day long. That quite reconciles me to what I must confess seems an imprudent engagement."

Carrie and I talked the matter over during the evening, and agreed that it did not always follow that an early engagement meant an unhappy marriage. Dear Carrie reminded me that we married early, and with the exception of a few trivial misunderstandings, we had never had a really serious word. I could not help thinking (as I told her) that half the pleasures of life were derived from the little struggles and small privations that one had to endure at the beginning of one's married life. Such struggles were generally occasioned by want of means, and often helped to make loving couples stand together all the firmer.

Carrie said I had expressed myself wonderfully well, and that I was quite a philosopher.

We are all vain at times, and I must confess I felt flattered by Carrie's little compliment.

I don't pretend to be able to express myself in fine language, but I feel I have the power of expressing my thoughts with simplicity and lucidness. About nine o'clock, to our surprise, Lupin entered, with a wild, reckless look, and in a hollow voice, which I must say seemed rather theatrical, said: "Have you any brandy?" I said: "No; but here is some whisky." Lupin drank off nearly a wineglassful without water, to my horror.

We all three sat reading in silence till ten, when Carrie and I rose to go to bed. Carrie said to Lupin: "I hope Daisy is well?"

Lupin, with a forced careless air that he must have picked up from the "Holloway Comedians," replied: "Oh, Daisy? You mean Miss Mutlar. I don't know whether she is well or not, but please *never to mention her name again in my presence.*"

WE HAVE A DOSE OF IRVING IMITATIONS.
MAKE THE ACQUAINTANCE OF A MR. PADGE.
DON'T CARE FOR HIM.   MR. BURWIN-
FOSSELTON BECOMES A NUISANCE.

CHAPTER XI

November 20. HAVE seen nothing of Lupin the whole day. Bought a cheap address-book. I spent the evening copying in the names and addresses of my friends and acquaintances. Left out the Mutlars of course.

November 21. Lupin turned up for a few minutes in the evening. He asked for a drop of brandy with a sort of careless look, which to my mind was theatrical and quite ineffective. I said : " My boy, I have none, and I don't think I should give it you if I had." Lupin said : " I'll go where I can get some," and walked out of the house. Carrie took the boy's part, and the rest of the evening was spent in a disagreeable discussion, in which the words " Daisy " and " Mutlar " must have occurred a thousand times.

November 22. Gowing and Cummings dropped in during the evening. Lupin also came in, bringing his friend, Mr. Burwin - Fosselton — one of the " Holloway Comedians "—who was at our party the other night, and who cracked our little round table. Happy to say Daisy Mutlar was never referred to. The conversation was almost entirely monopolised by the young fellow Fosselton, who not only looked rather like Mr. Irving, but seemed to

Mr. Burwin-Fosselton at supper.

imagine that he *was* the celebrated actor. I must say he gave some capital imitations of him. As he showed no signs of moving at supper time, I said : " If you like to stay, Mr. Fosselton, for our usual crust—pray do." He replied : " Oh ! thanks ; but please call me Burwin-Fosselton. It is a double name. There are lots of Fosseltons, but please call me Burwin-Fosselton."

He began doing the Irving business all through supper. He sank so low down in his chair that his chin was almost on a level with the table, and twice he kicked Carrie under the table, upset his wine, and flashed a knife uncomfortably near Gowing's face. After supper he kept stretching out his legs on the fender, indulging in scraps of quotations from plays which were Greek to me, and more than once knocked over the fire-irons, making a hideous row—poor Carrie already having a bad headache.

When he went, he said, to our surprise : " I will come to-morrow and bring my Irving make-up." Gowing and Cummings said they would like to see it and would come too. I could not help thinking they might as well give a party at my house while they are about it. However, as Carrie sensibly said : " Do anything, dear, to make Lupin forget the Daisy Mutlar business."

November 23. In the evening, Cummings came early. Gowing came a little later and brought, without asking permission, a fat and, I think, very vulgar-looking

Mr. Padge.

man named Padge, who appeared to be all moustache. Gowing never attempted any apology to either of us, but said Padge wanted to see the Irving business, to which Padge said : " That's right," and that is about all he *did* say during the entire evening. Lupin came in and seemed in much better spirits. He had prepared a bit of a surprise. Mr. Burwin-Fosselton had come in with him, but had gone upstairs to get ready. In half-an-hour Lupin retired from the parlour, and returning in a few minutes, announced " Mr. Henry Irving."

I must say we were all astounded. I never saw such a resemblance. It was astonishing. The only person who did not appear interested was the man Padge, who had got the best arm-chair, and was puffing away at a foul pipe into the fireplace. After some little time I said : " Why do actors always wear their hair so long ? " Carrie in a moment said, " Mr. Hare doesn't wear long *hair*." How we laughed except Mr. Fosselton, who said, in a rather patronising kind of way, " The joke, Mrs. Pooter, is extremely appropriate, if not altogether new." Thinking this rather a snub, I said : " Mr. Fosselton, I fancy —— " He interrupted me by saying : " Mr. *Burwin*-Fosselton, if you please," which made me quite forget what I was going to say to him. During the supper Mr. Burwin-Fosselton again monopolised the conversation with his Irving talk, and both Carrie and I came to the conclusion one can have even too much imitation of Irving. After supper,

Lupin announces "Mr. Henry Irving."

Mr. Burwin-Fosselton got a little too boisterous over his Irving imitation, and suddenly seizing Gowing by the collar of his coat, dug his thumb-nail, accidentally of course, into Gowing's neck and took a piece of flesh out. Gowing was rightly annoyed, but that man Padge, who having declined our modest supper in order that he should not lose his comfortable chair, burst into an uncontrollable fit of laughter at the little misadventure. I was so annoyed at the conduct of Padge, I said : " I suppose you would have laughed if he had poked Mr. Gowing's eye out ? " to which Padge replied : " That's right," and laughed more than ever. I think perhaps the greatest surprise was when we broke up, for Mr. Burwin-Fosselton said : " Good-night, Mr. Pooter. I'm glad you like the imitation, I'll bring *the other make-up to-morrow night.*"

November 24. I went to town without a pocket-handkerchief. This is the second time I have done this during the last week. I must be losing my memory. Had it not been for this Daisy Mutlar business, I would have written to Mr. Burwin-Fosselton and told him I should be *out* this evening, but I fancy he is the sort of young man who would come all the same.

Dear old Cummings came in the evening ; but Gowing sent round a little note saying he hoped I would excuse his not turning up, which rather amused me. He added that his neck was still painful. Of course, Burwin-Fosselton came, but Lupin never turned up, and imagine my utter disgust when that man Padge actually came again, and not even accompanied by Gowing. I was exasperated, and said : " Mr. Padge, this is a *surprise*." Dear Carrie, fearing unpleasantness, said : " Oh ! I suppose Mr. Padge has only come to see the other Irving make-up." Mr. Padge said : " That's right," and took the best chair again, from which he never moved the whole evening.

My only consolation is, he takes no supper, so he is not an expensive guest, but I shall speak to Gowing about the matter. The Irving imitations and conversations occupied the whole evening, till I was sick of it. Once we had a rather heated discussion, which was commenced by Cummings saying that it appeared to him that Mr. Burwin-Fosselton was not only *like* Mr. Irving, but was in his judgment every way as *good* or even *better*. I ventured to remark that after all it was but an imitation of an original.

Cummings said surely some imitations were better than the originals. I made what I considered a very clever remark : " Without an original there can be no imitation." Mr. Burwin-Fosselton said quite impertinently : " Don't discuss me in my presence, if you please ; and, Mr. Pooter, I should advise you to talk about what you understand ; " to which that cad Padge replied : " That's right." Dear Carrie saved the whole thing by suddenly saying : " I'll be Ellen Terry." Dear Carrie's imitation wasn't a bit liked, but she was so spontaneous and so funny that the disagreeable discussion passed off. When they left, I very pointedly said to Mr. Burwin-Fosselton and Mr. Padge that we should be engaged to-morrow evening.

November 25. Had a long letter from Mr. Fosselton respecting last night's Irving discussion. I was very angry, and I wrote and said I knew little or nothing about stage matters, was not in the least interested in them and positively declined to be drawn into a discussion on the subject, even at the risk of its leading to a breach of friendship. I never wrote a more determined letter.

On returning home at the usual hour on Saturday afternoon I met near the Archway Daisy Mutlar. My heart gave a leap. I bowed rather stiffly, but she affected not to have seen me. Very much annoyed in the evening by the laundress sending home an odd sock. Sarah said she sent two pairs, and the laundress declared only a pair and a half were sent. I spoke to Carrie about it, but she rather testily replied : " I am tired of speaking to her ; you had better go and speak to her yourself. She is outside." I did so, but the laundress declared that only an odd sock was sent.

Gowing passed into the passage at this time and was rude enough to listen to the conversation, and interrupting, said : " Don't waste the odd

sock, old man ; do an act of charity and give it
to some poor man with only one leg." The
laundress giggled like an idiot. I was disgusted
and walked upstairs for the purpose of pinning
down my collar, as the button had come off the
back of my shirt !

When I returned to the parlour, Gowing was
retailing his idiotic joke about the odd sock, and
Carrie was roaring with laughter. I suppose I
am losing my sense of humour. I spoke my
mind pretty freely about Padge. Gowing said he
had met him only once before that evening. He
had been introduced by a friend, and as he (Padge)
had " stood " a good dinner, Gowing wished to
show him some little return. Upon my word,
Gowing's coolness surpasses all belief. Lupin
came in before I could reply, and Gowing
unfortunately inquired after Daisy Mutlar. Lupin
shouted : " Mind your own business, sir ! " and
bounced out of the room, slamming the door.
The remainder of the night was Daisy Mutlar—
Daisy Mutlar—Daisy Mutlar. Oh dear !

November 26,
Sunday.
The Curate preached a very good
sermon to-day—very good indeed.
His appearance is never so impressive as our dear old Vicar's,
but I am bound to say his sermons are much more
impressive. A rather annoying incident occurred,
of which I must make mention. Mrs. Fernlosse,
who is quite a grand lady, living in one of those
large houses in the Camden Road, stopped to

speak to me after church, when we were all coming out. I must say I felt flattered, for she is thought a good deal of. I suppose she knew me through seeing me so often take round the plate, especially as she always occupies the corner seat of the pew. She is a very influential lady, and may have had something of the utmost importance to say, but unfortunately, as she commenced to speak a strong gust of wind came and blew my hat off into the middle of the road.

I had to run after it, and had the greatest difficulty in recovering it. When I had succeeded in doing so, I found Mrs. Fernlosse had walked on with some swell friends, and I felt I could not well approach her now, especially as my hat was smothered with mud. I cannot say how disappointed I felt.

In the evening (*Sunday* evening of all others) I found an impertinent note from Mr. Burwin-Fosselton, which ran as follows :

" DEAR MR. POOTER,—Although your junior by perhaps some twenty or thirty years—which is sufficient reason that you ought to have a longer record of the things and ways in this miniature of a planet—I feel it is just within the bounds of possibility that the wheels of *your* life don't travel so quickly round as those of the humble writer of these lines. The dandy horse of past days has been known to overtake the *slow coach*.

" Do I make myself understood ?

" Very well, then ! Permit me, Mr. Pooter,

to advise you to accept the *verb. sap.* Acknowledge your defeat, and take your whipping gracefully ; for remember *you* threw down the glove, and I cannot claim to be either mentally or physically a *coward !*

"*Revenons à nos moutons.*

"Our lives run in different grooves. I live for MY ART—THE STAGE. Your life is devoted to commercial pursuits—'A life among Ledgers.' My books are of different metal. Your life in the City is honourable, I admit. *But how different !* Cannot even you see the ocean between us ? A channel that prevents the meeting of our brains in harmonious accord. Ah ! But *chaçun à son goût.*

"I have registered a vow to mount the steps of fame. I may crawl, I may slip, I may even falter (we are all weak), but *reach the top rung of the ladder I will ! ! !* When there, my voice shall be heard, for I will shout to the multitudes below : '*Vici !*' For the present I am only an amateur, and my work is unknown, forsooth, save to a party of friends, with here and there an enemy.

"But, Mr. Pooter, let me ask you, 'What is the difference between the amateur and the professional ? '

"None ! ! !

"Stay ! Yes, there is a difference. One is *paid* for doing what the other does as skilfully for *nothing !*

"But *I* will be *paid*, too ! For *I*, contrary to

the wishes of my family and friends, have at last elected to adopt the stage as *my* profession. And when the *farce* craze is over—*and, mark you, that will be soon*—I will make my power known; for I feel—pardon my apparent conceit—that there is no living man who can play the hump-backed Richard as I *feel* and *know* I can.

"And *you* will be the first to come round and bend your head in submission. There are many matters you may understand, but knowledge of the fine art of acting is to you an *unknown quantity*.

"Pray let this discussion cease with this letter. *Vale !*

"Yours truly,

"BURWIN-FOSSELTON."

I was disgusted. When Lupin came in, I handed him this impertinent letter, and said: "My boy, in that letter you can see the true character of your friend."

Lupin, to my surprise, said: "Oh yes. He showed me the letter before he sent it. I think he is right, and you ought to apologise."

A SERIOUS DISCUSSION CONCERNING THE
USE AND VALUE OF MY DIARY.
LUPIN'S OPINION OF 'XMAS. LUPIN'S
UNFORTUNATE ENGAGEMENT IS ON AGAIN.

CHAPTER XII

As I open my scribbling diary I *December* 17. find the words " Oxford Michaelmas Term ends." Why this should induce me to indulge in retrospective I don't know, but it does. The last few weeks of my diary are of minimum interest. The breaking off of the engagement between Lupin and Daisy Mutlar has made him a different being, and Carrie a rather depressing companion. She was a little dull last Saturday, and I thought to cheer her up by reading some extracts from my diary ; but she walked out of the room in the middle of the reading, without a word. On her return, I said : " Did my diary bore you, darling ? "

She replied, to my surprise : " I really wasn't listening, dear. I was obliged to leave to give instructions to the laundress. In consequence of some stuff she puts in the water, two more of Lupin's coloured shirts have run ; and he says he won't wear them."

I said : " Everything is Lupin. It's all Lupin, Lupin, Lupin. There was not a single button on *my* shirt yesterday, but *I* made no complaint."

Carrie simply replied : " You should do as all other men do, and wear studs. In fact, I never saw anyone but you wear buttons on the shirt-fronts."

I said : " I certainly wore none yesterday, for there were none on."

Another thought that strikes me is that Gowing seldom calls in the evening, and Cummings never does. I fear they don't get on well with Lupin.

December 18. Yesterday I was in a retrospective vein—to-day it is *prospective*. I see nothing but clouds, clouds, clouds. Lupin is perfectly intolerable over the Daisy Mutlar business. He won't say what is the cause of the breach. He is evidently condemning her conduct, and yet, if we venture to agree with him, says he won't hear a word against her. So what is one to do ? Another thing which is disappointing to me is, that Carrie and Lupin take no interest whatever in my diary.

I broached the subject at the breakfast-table to-day. I said : " I was in hopes that, if anything ever happened to me, the diary would be an endless source of pleasure to you both ; to say nothing of the chance of the remuneration which may accrue from its being published."

Both Carrie and Lupin burst out laughing. Carrie was sorry for this, I could see, for she said : " I did not mean to be rude, dear Charlie ; but *truly* I do not think your diary would sufficiently interest the public to be taken up by a publisher."

I replied : " I am sure it would prove quite as interesting as some of the ridiculous reminiscences that have been published lately.

Besides, it's the diary that makes the man. Where would Evelyn and Pepys have been if it had not been for their diaries?"

Carrie said I was quite a philosopher; but Lupin, in a jeering tone, said: "If it had been written on larger paper, Guv., we might get a fair price from a butterman for it."

As I am in the prospective vein, I vow the end of this year will see the end of my diary.

December 19. The annual invitation came to spend Christmas with Carrie's mother— the usual family festive gathering to which we always look forward. Lupin declined to go. I was astounded, and expressed my surprise and disgust. Lupin then obliged us with the following Radical speech: "I hate a family gathering at Christmas. What does it mean? Why someone says: 'Ah! we miss poor Uncle James, who was here last year,' and we all begin to snivel. Someone else says: 'It's two years since poor Aunt Liz used to sit in that corner.' Then we all begin to snivel again. Then another gloomy relation says: 'Ah! I wonder whose turn it will be next?' Then we all snivel again, and proceed to eat and drink too much; and they don't discover until *I* get up that we have been seated thirteen at dinner."

December 20. Went to Smirksons', the drapers, in the Strand, who this year have turned out everything in the shop and devoted the whole place to the sale of Christmas cards. Shop crowded with people, who seemed to take up the cards rather roughly, and, after a hurried glance at them, throw them down again. I remarked to one of the young persons serving, that carelessness appeared to be a disease with some purchasers. The observation was scarcely out of my mouth, when my thick coat-sleeve caught against a large pile of expensive cards in boxes one on top of the other, and threw them down. The manager came forward, looking very much annoyed, and picking up several cards from the ground, said to one of the assistants, with a palpable side-glance at me : " Put these amongst the sixpenny goods ; they can't be sold for a shilling now." The result was, I felt it my duty to buy some of these damaged cards.

I had to buy more and pay more than intended. Unfortunately I did not examine them all, and when I got home I discovered a vulgar card with a picture of a fat nurse with two babies, one black and the other white, and the words : " We wish Pa a Merry Christmas." I tore up the card and threw it away. Carrie said the great disadvantage of going out in Society and increasing the number of our friends was, that we should have to send out nearly two dozen cards this year.

December 21. To save the postman a miserable Christmas, we follow the example of all unselfish people, and send out our cards early. Most of the cards had finger-marks, which I did not notice at night. I shall buy all future cards in the daytime. Lupin (who, ever since he has had the appointment with a stock and share broker, does not seem over-scrupulous in his dealings) told me never to rub out the pencilled price on the backs of the cards. I asked him why. Lupin said : " Suppose your card is marked 9d. Well, all you have to do is to pencil a 3—and a long down-stroke after it—in *front* of the ninepence, and people will think you have given five times the price for it."

In the evening Lupin was very low-spirited, and I reminded him that behind the clouds the sun was shining. He said : " Ugh ! it never shines on me." I said : " Stop, Lupin, my boy ; you are worried about Daisy Mutlar. Don't think of her any more. You ought to congratulate yourself on having got off a very bad bargain. Her notions are far too grand for our simple tastes." He jumped up and said : " I won't allow one word to be uttered against her. She's worth the whole bunch of your friends put together, that inflated, sloping-head of a Perkupp included." I left the room with silent dignity, but caught my foot in the mat.

December 23. I exchanged no words with Lupin in the morning ; but as he seemed to be in exuberant spirits in the evening, I ventured to ask him where he intended to spend his Christmas. He replied : " Oh, most likely at the Mutlars'. "

*F

In wonderment, I said: "What! after your engagement has been broken off?"

Lupin said: "Who said it is off?"

I said: "You have given us both to understand——"

He interrupted me by saying: "Well, never mind what I said. *It is on again—there!*"

I RECEIVE AN INSULTING CHRISTMAS
CARD. WE SPEND A PLEASANT CHRISTMAS
AT CARRIE'S MOTHER'S. A MR. MOSS
IS RATHER TOO FREE. A BOISTEROUS
EVENING, DURING WHICH I AM STRUCK IN
THE DARK. I RECEIVE AN EXTRAORDINARY
LETTER FROM MR. MUTLAR, SENIOR,
RESPECTING LUPIN. WE MISS DRINKING
OUT THE OLD YEAR.

CHAPTER XIII

December 24. I AM a poor man, but I would gladly give ten shillings to find out who sent me the insulting Christmas card I received this morning. I never insult people ; why should they insult me ? The worst part of the transaction is, that I find myself suspecting all my friends. The handwriting on the envelope is evidently disguised, being written sloping the wrong way. I cannot think either Gowing or Cummings would do such a mean thing. Lupin denied all knowledge of it, and I believe him ; although I disapprove of his laughing and sympathising with the offender. Mr. Franching would be above such an act ; and I don't think any of the Mutlars would descend to such a course. I wonder if Pitt, that impudent clerk at the office, did it ? Or Mrs. Birrell, the charwoman, or Burwin-Fosselton ? The writing is too good for the former.

Christmas Day. We caught the 10.20 train at Paddington, and spent a pleasant day at Carrie's mother's. The country was quite nice and pleasant, although the roads were sloppy. We dined in the middle of the day, just ten of us, and talked over old times. If everybody had a nice, *un*interfering mother-in-law, such as I have, what a deal of happiness there would be in the world. Being all in good spirits, I proposed her health; and I made, I think, a very good speech.

I concluded, rather neatly, by saying: "On an occasion like this—whether relatives, friends, or acquaintances,—we are all inspired with good feelings towards each other. We are of one mind, and think only of love and friendship. Those who have quarrelled with absent friends should kiss and make it up. Those who happily have *not* fallen out, can kiss all the same."

I saw the tears in the eyes of both Carrie and her mother, and must say I felt very flattered by the compliment. That dear old Reverend John Panzy Smith, who married us, made a most cheerful and amusing speech, and said he should act on my suggestion respecting the kissing. He then walked round the table and kissed all the ladies, including Carrie. Of course one did not object to this; but I was more than staggered when a young fellow named Moss, who was a stranger to me, and who had scarcely spoken a word through dinner, jumped up suddenly with a sprig of misletoe, and exclaimed: "Hulloh! I don't see why I shouldn't be on in this scene." Before one could realise what he was about to do, he kissed Carrie and the rest of the ladies.

Fortunately the matter was treated as a joke, and we all laughed: but it was a dangerous experiment, and I felt very uneasy for a moment as to the result. I subsequently referred to the matter to Carrie, but she said : "Oh, he's not much more than a boy." I said that he had a very large moustache for a boy. Carrie replied : " I didn't say he was not a nice boy."

December 26. I did not sleep very well last night ; I never do in a strange bed. I feel a little indigestion, which one must expect at this time of the year. Carrie and I returned to Town in the evening. Lupin came in late. He said he enjoyed his Christmas, and added : " I feel as fit as a Lowther Arcade fiddle, and only require a little more ' oof ' to feel as fit as a £500 Stradivarius." I have long since given up trying to understand Lupin's slang, or asking him to explain it.

December 27. I told Lupin I was expecting Gowing and Cummings to drop in to-morrow evening for a quiet game. I was in hope the boy would volunteer to stay in, and help to amuse them. Instead of which, he said : " Oh, you had better put them off, as I have asked Daisy and Frank Mutlar to come." I said I could not think of doing such a thing. Lupin said : " Then I will send a wire, and put off Daisy." I suggested that a post-card or letter would reach her quite soon enough, and would not be so extravagant.

Carrie, who had listened to the above conversation with apparent annoyance, directed a well-aimed shaft at Lupin. She said : " Lupin, why do you object to Daisy meeting your father's friends ? Is it because they are not good enough for her, or (which is equally possible) *she* is not good enough for them ? " Lupin was dumbfounded, and could make no reply. When he left the room, I gave Carrie a kiss of approval.

December 28.   Lupin, on coming down to breakfast, said to his mother : " I have not put off Daisy and Frank, and should like them to join Gowing and Cummings this evening." I felt very pleased with the boy for this. Carrie said, in reply : " I am glad you let me know in time, as I can turn over the cold leg of mutton, dress it with a little parsley, and no one will know it has been cut." She further said she would make a few custards, and stew some pippins, so that they would be cold by the evening.

Finding Lupin in good spirits, I asked him quietly if he really had any personal objection to either Gowing or Cummings. He replied : " Not in the least. I think Cummings looks rather an ass, but that is partly due to his patronising ' the three-and-six-one-price hat company,' and wearing a reach-me-down frock-coat. As for that perpetual brown velveteen jacket of Gowing's — why, he resembles an itinerant photographer."

I said it was not the coat that made the gentleman ; whereupon Lupin, with a laugh, replied : " No, and it wasn't much of a gentleman who made their coats."

We were rather jolly at supper, and Daisy made herself very agreeable, especially in the earlier part of the evening, when she sang. At supper, however, she said : " Can you make tee-to-tums with bread ? " and she commenced rolling up pieces of bread, and twisting them round on the table. I felt this to be bad manners, but of course said nothing. Presently Daisy and Lupin, to my disgust, began throwing bread-pills at each other. Frank followed suit, and so did Cummings and Gowing, to my astonishment. They then commenced throwing hard pieces of crust, one piece catching me on the forehead, and making me blink. I said : " Steady, please ; steady ! " Frank jumped up and said : " Tum, tum ; then the band played."

I did not know what this meant, but they all roared, and continued the bread-battle. Gowing suddenly seized all the parsley off the cold mutton, and threw it full in my face. I looked daggers at Gowing, who replied : " I say, it's no good trying to look indignant, with your hair full of parsley." I rose from the table, and insisted that a stop should be put to this foolery at once. Frank Mutlar shouted : " Time, gentlemen, please ! time ! " and turned out the gas, leaving us in absolute darkness.

I was feeling my way out of the room, when I suddenly received a hard intentional punch at the back of my head. I said loudly : " Who did that ? " There was no answer ; so I repeated the question, with the same result. I struck a match, and lighted the gas. They were all talking and laughing, so I kept my own counsel; but, after they had gone, I said to Carrie : " The person who sent me that insulting post-card at Christmas was here to-night."

December 29. I had a most vivid dream last night. I woke up, and on falling asleep, dreamed the same dream over again precisely. I dreamt I heard Frank Mutlar telling his sister that he had not only sent me the insulting Christmas card, but admitted that he was the one who punched my head last night in the dark. As fate would have it, Lupin, at breakfast, was reading extracts from a letter he had just received from Frank.

I asked him to pass the envelope, that I might compare the writing. He did so, and I examined it by the side of the envelope containing the Christmas card. I detected a similarity in the writing, in spite of the attempted disguise. I passed them on to Carrie, who began to laugh. I asked her what she was laughing at, and she said the card was never directed to me at all. It was " L. Pooter," not " C. Pooter." Lupin asked to look at the direction and the card, and exclaimed, with a laugh : " Oh yes, Guv., it's meant for me." I said : " Are you in the habit of receiving insulting Christmas cards ? " He replied : " Oh yes, and of *sending* them, too."

In the evening Gowing called, and said he enjoyed himself very much last night. I took the opportunity to confide in him, as an old friend, about the vicious punch last night. He burst out laughing, and said : " Oh, it was *your head*, was it ? I know I accidentally hit something, but I thought it was a brick wall." I told him I felt hurt, in both senses of the expression.

December 30, *Sunday*. Lupin spent the whole day with the Mutlars. He seemed rather cheerful in the evening, so I said : " I'm glad to see you so happy, Lupin." He answered : " Well, Daisy is a splendid girl, but I was obliged to take her old fool of a father down a peg. What with his meanness over his cigars, his stinginess over his drinks, his farthing economy in turning down the gas if you only quit the room for a second, writing to one on half-sheets of note-paper, sticking the remnant of the last cake of soap on to the new cake, putting two bricks on each side of the fireplace, and his general ' outside-halfpenny-'bus-ness,' I was compelled to let him have a bit of my mind." I said : " Lupin, you are not much more than a boy ; I hope you won't repent it."

December 31. The last day of the Old Year. I received an extraordinary letter from Mr. Mutlar, senior. He writes : " Dear Sir,—For a long time past I have had considerable difficulty deciding the important question, ' Who is the master of my own house ? Myself, or *your son* Lupin ? ' Believe me, I have no prejudice one way or the other; but I have been most reluctantly compelled to give judgment to the effect that *I* am the master of it. Under the circumstances, it has become my duty to forbid your son to enter my house again. I am sorry, because it deprives me of the society of one of the most modest, unassuming, and gentlemanly persons I have ever had the honour of being acquainted with."

I did not desire the last day to wind up disagreeably, so I said nothing to either Carrie or Lupin about the letter.

A most terrible fog came on, and Lupin would go out in it, but promised to be back to drink out the Old Year—a custom we have always observed. At a quarter to twelve Lupin had not returned, and the fog was fearful. As time was drawing close, I got out the spirits. Carrie and I deciding on whisky, I opened a fresh bottle; but Carrie said it smelt like brandy. As I knew it to be whisky, I said there was nothing to discuss. Carrie, evidently vexed that Lupin had not come in, *did* discuss it all the same, and wanted me to have a small wager with her to decide by the smell. I said I could decide it by the taste in a moment. A silly and unnecessary argument followed, the result of which was we suddenly saw it was a quarter - past twelve, and, for the first time in our married life, we missed welcoming in the New Year. Lupin got home at a quarter-past two, having got lost in the fog—so he said.

BEGIN THE YEAR WITH AN UNEXPECTED
PROMOTION AT THE OFFICE.   I MAKE TWO
GOOD JOKES.   I GET AN ENORMOUS RISE
IN   MY   SALARY.   LUPIN   SPECULATES
SUCCESSFULLY AND STARTS A PONY-TRAP.
HAVE TO SPEAK TO SARAH.   EXTRAORDINARY
CONDUCT   OF   GOWING'S.

CHAPTER XIV

January 1. I HAD intended concluding my diary ast week; but a most important event has happened, so I shall continue for a little while longer on the fly-leaves attached to the end of my last year's diary. It had just struck half-past one, and I was on the point of leaving the office to have my dinner, when I received a message that Mr. Perkupp desired to see me at once. I must confess that my heart commenced to beat and I had most serious misgivings.

Mr. Perkupp was in his room writing, and he said: "Take a seat, Mr. Pooter, I shall not be a moment."

I replied: "No, thank you, sir; I'll stand." I watched the clock on the mantelpiece, and I was waiting quite twenty minutes; but it seemed hours. Mr. Perkupp at last got up himself.

I said: "I hope there is nothing wrong, sir?"

He replied: "Oh dear, no! quite the reverse, I hope." What a weight off my mind! My breath seemed to come back again in an instant.

Mr. Perkupp said: "Mr. Buckling is going to retire, and there will be some slight changes in the office. You have been with us nearly twenty-one years, and, in consequence of your conduct during that period, we intend making a special promotion in your favour. We have not quite decided how you will be placed; but in any case there will be a considerable increase in your salary, which, it is quite unnecessary for me to say, you fully deserve. I have an appointment at two; but you shall hear more to-morrow."

He then left the room quickly, and I was not even allowed time or thought to express a single word of grateful thanks to him. I need not say how dear Carrie received this joyful news. With perfect simplicity she said: "At last we shall be able to have a chimney-glass for the back drawing-room, which we always wanted." I added: "Yes, and at last you shall have that little costume which you saw at Peter Robinson's so cheap."

January 2. I was in a great state of suspense all day at the office. I did not like to worry Mr. Perkupp; but as he did not send for me, and mentioned yesterday that he would see me again to-day, I thought it better, perhaps, to go to him. I knocked at his door, and on entering, Mr. Perkupp said: "Oh! it's you, Mr. Pooter; do you want to see me?" I said: "No, sir, I thought you wanted to see me!" "Oh!" he replied, "I remember. Well, I am very busy to-day; I will see you to-morrow."

January 3. Still in a state of anxiety and excitement, which was not alleviated by ascertaining that Mr. Perkupp sent word he should not be at the office to-day. In the evening, Lupin, who was busily engaged with a paper, said suddenly to me : " Do you know anything about *chalk pits*, Guv. ? " I said : " No, my boy, not that I'm aware of." Lupin said : " Well, I give you the tip ; *chalk pits* are as safe as Consols, and pay six per cent. at par." I said a rather neat thing, viz. : " They may be six per cent. at *par*, but your *pa* has no money to invest." Carrie and I both roared with laughter. Lupin did not take the slightest notice of the joke, although I purposely repeated it for him ; but continued : " I give you the tip, that's all—*chalk pits !* " I said another funny thing : " Mind you don't fall into them ! " Lupin put on a supercilious smile, and said : " Bravo ! Joe Miller."

January 4.   Mr. Perkupp sent for me and told me that my position would be that of one of the senior clerks. I was more than overjoyed. Mr. Perkupp added, he would let me know to-morrow what the salary would be. This means another day's anxiety ; I don't mind, for it is anxiety of the right sort. That reminded me that I had forgotten to speak to Lupin about the letter I received from Mr. Mutlar, senr. I broached the subject to Lupin in the evening, having first consulted Carrie. Lupin was riveted to the *Financial News*, as if he had been a born capitalist, and I said : " Pardon me a moment, Lupin, how is it you have not been to the Mutlars' any day this week ? "

Lupin answered : " I told you ! I cannot stand old Mutlar."

I said : " Mr. Mutlar writes to me to say pretty plainly that he cannot stand you ! "

Lupin said : " Well, I like his cheek in writing to *you*. I'll find out if his father is still alive, and I will write *him* a note complaining of *his* son, and I'll state pretty clearly that his son is a blithering idiot ! "

I said : " Lupin, please moderate your expressions in the presence of your mother."

Lupin said : " I'm very sorry, but there is no other expression one can apply to him. However, I'm determined not to enter his place again."

I said : " You know, Lupin, he has forbidden you the house."

Lupin replied : " Well, we won't split straws— it's all the same. Daisy is a trump, and will wait for me ten years, if necessary."

January 5.
I can scarcely write the news. Mr. Perkupp told me my salary would be raised £100 ! I stood gaping for a moment unable to realise it. I annually get £10 rise, and I thought it might be £15 or even £20 ; but £100 surpasses all belief. Carrie and I both rejoiced over our good fortune. Lupin came home in the evening in the utmost good spirits. I sent Sarah quietly round to the grocer's for a bottle of champagne, the same as we had before, " Jackson Frères." It was opened at supper, and I said to Lupin : " This is to celebrate

some good news I have received to-day." Lupin replied : " Hooray, Guv. ! And I have some good news, also ; a double event, eh ? " I said : " My boy, as a result of twenty-one years' industry and strict attention to the interests of my superiors in office, I have been rewarded with promotion and a rise in salary of £100."

Lupin gave three cheers, and we rapped the table furiously, which brought in Sarah to see what the matter was. Lupin ordered us to " fill up " again, and addressing us upstanding, said : " Having been in the firm of Job Cleanands, stock and share-brokers, a few weeks, and *not* having paid particular attention to the interests of my superiors in office, my Guv'nor, as a reward to me, allotted me £5 worth of shares in a really good thing. The result is, to-day I have made £200." I said : " Lupin, you are joking." " No, Guv., it's the good old truth ; Job Cleanands *put me on to Chlorates.*"

January 21. I am very much concerned at Lupin having started a pony-trap. I said : " Lupin, are you justified in this outrageous extravagance ? " Lupin replied : " Well, one must get to the City somehow. I've only hired it, and can give it up any time I like." I repeated my question : " Are you justified in this extravagance ? " He replied : " Look here, Guv. ; excuse me saying so, but you're a bit out of date. It does not pay nowadays, fiddling about over small things. I don't mean anything personal,

Guv'nor. My boss says if I take his tip, and stick to big things, I can make big money!" I said I thought the very idea of speculation most horrifying. Lupin said: "It is not speculation, it's a dead cert." I advised him, at all events, not to continue the pony and cart; but he replied: "I made £200 in one day; now suppose I only make £200 in a month, or put it at £100 a month, which is ridiculously low—why, that is £1,250 a year. What's a few pounds a week for a trap?"

I did not pursue the subject further, beyond saying that I should feel glad when the autumn came, and Lupin would be of age and responsible for his own debts. He answered: "My dear Guv., I promise you faithfully that I will never speculate with what I have not got. I shall only go on Job Cleanands' tips, and as he is in the 'know' it is pretty safe sailing." I felt somewhat relieved. Gowing called in the evening and, to my surprise, informed me that, as he had made £10 by one of Lupin's tips, he intended asking us and the Cummings round next Saturday. Carrie and I said we should be delighted.

January 22. I don't generally lose my temper with servants; but I had to speak to Sarah rather sharply about a careless habit she has recently contracted of shaking the table-cloth, after removing the breakfast things, in a manner which causes all the crumbs to fall on the carpet, eventually to be trodden in. Sarah answered very rudely: "Oh, you are always complaining." I replied : " Indeed, I am not. I spoke to you last week about walking all over the drawing-room carpet with a piece of yellow soap on the heel of your boot." She said : " And you're always grumbling about your breakfast." I said : " No, I am not ; but I feel perfectly justified in complaining that I never can get a hard-boiled egg. The moment I crack the shell it spurts all over the plate, and I have spoken to you at least fifty times about it." She began to cry and make a scene ; but fortunately my 'bus came by, so I had a good excuse for leaving her. Gowing left a message in the evening, that we were not to forget next Saturday. Carrie amusingly said : " As he has never asked any friends before, we are not likely to forget it."

January 23. I asked Lupin to try and change the hard brushes, he recently made me a present of, for some softer ones, as my hairdresser tells me I ought not to brush my hair too much just now.

January 24. The new chimney-glass came home for the back drawing-room. Carrie arranged some fans very prettily on the top and on each side. It is an immense improvement to the room.

January 25. We had just finished our tea, when who should come in but Cummings, who has not been here for over three weeks. I noticed that he looked anything but well, so I said: "Well, Cummings, how are you? You look a little blue." He replied: "Yes! and I feel blue too." I said: "Why, what's the matter?" He said: "Oh, nothing, except that I have been on my back for a couple of weeks, that's all. At one time my doctor nearly gave me up, yet not a soul has come near me. No one has even taken the trouble to inquire whether I was alive or dead."

I said: "This is the first I have heard of it. I have passed your house several nights, and presumed you had company, as the rooms were so brilliantly lighted."

Cummings replied: "No! The only company I have had was my wife, the doctor, and the landlady—the last-named having turned out a perfect trump. I wonder you did not see it in the paper. I know it was mentioned in the *Bicycle News*."

I thought to cheer him up, and said: "Well, you are all right now?"

He replied: "That's not the question. The question is whether an illness does not enable you to discover who are your *true* friends."

I said such an observation was unworthy of him. To make matters worse, in came Gowing, who gave Cummings a violent slap on the back, and said: "Hulloh! Have you seen a ghost? You look scared to death, like Irving in *Macbeth*." I said: "Gently, Gowing, the poor fellow has been very ill." Gowing roared with laughter and said:

" Yes, and you look it, too." Cummings quietly said : " Yes, and I feel it too—not that I suppose you care."

An awkward silence followed. Gowing said : " Never mind, Cummings, you and the missis come round to my place to-morrow, and it will cheer you up a bit ; for we'll open a bottle of wine."

An extraordinary thing happened.

January 26.   Carrie and I went round to Gowing's, as arranged, at half-past seven. We knocked and rang several times without getting an answer. At last the latch was drawn and the door opened a little way, the chain still being up. A man in shirt-sleeves put his head through and said : " Who is it ? What do you want ? "   I said : " Mr. Gowing, he is expecting us." The man said (as well as I could hear, owing to the yapping of a little dog) : " I don't think he is. Mr. Gowing is not at home." I said : " He will be in directly."

With that observation he slammed the door, leaving Carrie and me standing on the steps with a cutting wind blowing round the corner.

Carrie advised me to knock again. I did so, and then discovered for the first time that the knocker had been newly painted, and the paint had come off on my gloves—which were, in consequence, completely spoiled.

I knocked at the door with my stick two or three times.

The man opened the door, taking the chain off this time, and began abusing me. He said : " What do you mean by scratching the paint with your stick like that, spoiling the varnish ? You ought to be ashamed of yourself."

I said : " Pardon me, Mr. Gowing invited —— "

He interrupted and said : " I don't care for Mr. Gowing, or any of his friends. This is *my* door, not Mr. Gowing's. There are people here besides Mr. Gowing."

The impertinence of this man was nothing. I scarcely noticed it, it was so trivial in comparison with the scandalous conduct of Gowing.

At this moment Cummings and his wife arrived. Cummings was very lame and leaning on a stick ; but got up the steps and asked what the matter was.

The man said : " Mr. Gowing said nothing about expecting anyone. All he said was he had just received an invitation to Croydon, and he should not be back till Monday evening. He took his bag with him."

With that he slammed the door again. I was too indignant with Gowing's conduct to say anything. Cummings looked white with rage, and as he descended the steps struck his stick violently on the ground and said : " Scoundrel ! "

GOWING EXPLAINS HIS CONDUCT. LUPIN
TAKES US FOR A DRIVE, WHICH WE
DON'T ENJOY. LUPIN INTRODUCES US
TO MR. MURRAY POSH.

G

CHAPTER XV

February 8.   It does seem hard I cannot get good sausages for breakfast. They are either full of bread or spice, or are as red as beef. Still anxious about the £20 I invested last week by Lupin's advice. However, Cummings has done the same.

February 9.   Exactly a fortnight has passed, and I have neither seen nor heard from Gowing respecting his extraordinary conduct in asking us round to his house, and then being out. In the evening Carrie was engaged marking a half-dozen new collars I had purchased. I'll back Carrie's marking against anybody's. While I was drying them at the fire, and Carrie was rebuking me for scorching them, Cummings came in.

He seemed quite well again, and chaffed us about marking the collars. I asked him if he had heard from Gowing, and he replied that he had not. I said I should not have believed that Gowing could have acted in such an ungentlemanly manner. Cummings said : " You are mild in your description of him ; I think he has acted like a cad."

The words were scarcely out of his mouth when the door opened, and Gowing, putting in his head, said : " May I come in ? " I said : " Certainly."

Carrie said very pointedly : "Well, you *are* a stranger." Gowing said : "Yes, I've been on and off to Croydon during the last fortnight." I could see Cummings was boiling over, and eventually he tackled Gowing very strongly respecting his conduct last Saturday week. Gowing appeared surprised, and said : "Why, I posted a letter to you in the morning announcing that the party was ' off, very much off.' " I said : "I never got it." Gowing, turning to Carrie, said : "I suppose letters sometimes *miscarry*, don't they, *Mrs.* Carrie ? " Cummings sharply said : "This is not a time for joking. *I* had no notice of the party being put off." Gowing replied : "I told Pooter in my note to tell you, as I was in a hurry. However, I'll inquire at the post-office, and we must meet again at my place." I added that I hoped he would be present at the next meeting. Carrie roared at this, and even Cummings could not help laughing.

February 10,
Sunday.
Contrary to my wishes, Carrie allowed Lupin to persuade her to take her for a drive in the afternoon in his trap. I quite disapprove of driving on a Sunday, but I did not like to trust Carrie alone with Lupin, so I offered to go too. Lupin said : "Now, that is nice of you, Guv., but you won't mind sitting on the back-seat of the cart ? "

Lupin proceeded to put on a bright-blue coat that seemed miles too large for him. Carrie said it wanted taking in considerably at the back. Lupin said : " Haven't you seen a box-coat before ? You can't drive in anything else."

He may wear what he likes in the future, for I shall never drive with him again. His conduct was shocking. When we passed Highgate Archway, he tried to pass everything and everybody. He shouted to respectable people who were walking quietly in the road to get out of the way ; he flicked at the horse of an old man who was riding, causing it to rear ; and, as I had to ride backwards, I was compelled to face a gang of roughs in a donkey-cart, whom Lupin had chaffed, and who turned and followed us for nearly a mile, bellowing, indulging in coarse jokes and laughter, to say nothing of occasionally pelting us with orange-peel.

Lupin's excuse—that the Prince of Wales would have to put up with the same sort of thing if he drove to the Derby—was of little consolation to either Carrie or myself. Frank Mutlar called in the evening, and Lupin went out with him.

February 11. Feeling a little concerned about Lupin, I mustered up courage to speak to Mr. Perkupp about him. Mr. Perkupp has always been most kind to me, so I told him everything, including yesterday's adventure. Mr. Perkupp kindly replied : " There is no necessity for you to be anxious, Mr. Pooter. It would be impossible for a son of such good parents to turn out erroneously. Remember he is young, and will soon get older. I wish we could find room for him in this firm." The advice of this good man takes loads off my mind. In the evening Lupin came in.

After our little supper, he said : " My dear parents, I have some news, which I fear will affect you considerably." I felt a qualm come over me, and said nothing. Lupin then said : " It may distress you—in fact, I'm sure it will—but this afternoon I have given up my pony and trap for ever." It may seem absurd but I was so pleased, I immediately opened a bottle of port. Gowing dropped in just in time, bringing with him a large sheet, with a print of a tailless donkey, which he fastened against the wall. He then produced several separate tails, and we spent the remainder of the evening trying blindfolded to pin a tail on in the proper place. My sides positively ached with laughter when I went to bed.

In the evening I spoke to Lupin *February* 12. about his engagement with Daisy Mutlar. I asked if he had heard from her. He replied : " No ; she promised that old windbag of a father of hers that she would not communicate with me. I see Frank Mutlar, of course ; in fact, he said he might call again this evening." Frank called, but said he could not stop, as he had a friend waiting outside for him, named Murray Posh, adding he was quite a swell. Carrie asked Frank to bring him in.

He was brought in, Gowing entering at the same

Mr. Murray Posh.

time. Mr. Murray Posh was a tall, fat young man, and was evidently of a very nervous disposition, as he subsequently confessed he would never go in a hansom cab, nor would he enter a four-wheeler until the driver had first got on the box with his reins in his hands.

On being introduced, Gowing, with his usual want of tact, said : " Any relation to ' Posh's three-shilling hats ' ? " Mr. Posh replied : " Yes ; but please understand I don't try on hats myself. I take no *active* part in the business." I replied : " I wish I had a business like it." Mr. Posh seemed pleased, and gave a long but most interesting history of the extraordinary difficulties in the manufacture of cheap hats.

Murry Posh evidently knew Daisy Mutlar very intimately from the way he was talking of her ; and Frank said to Lupin once, laughingly : " If you don't look out, Posh will cut you out ! " When they had all gone, I referred to this flippant conversation ; and Lupin said, sarcastically : " A man who is jealous has no respect for himself. A man who would be jealous of an elephant like Murray Post could only have a contempt for himself. I know Daisy. She *would* wait ten years for me, as I said before ; in fact, if necessary, *she would wait twenty years for me.*"

WE LOSE MONEY OVER LUPIN'S ADVICE AS
TO INVESTMENT, SO DOES CUMMINGS.
MURRAY POSH ENGAGED TO DAISY MUTLAR.

CHAPTER XVI

February 18. Carrie has several times recently called attention to the thinness of my hair at the top of my head, and recommended me to get it seen to. I was this morning trying to look at it by the aid of a small hand-glass, when somehow my elbow caught against the edge of the chest of drawers and knocked the glass out of my hand and smashed it. Carrie was in an awful way about it, as she is rather absurdly superstitious. To make matters worse, my large photograph in the drawing-room fell during the night, and the glass cracked.

Carrie said : " Mark my words, Charles, some misfortune is about to happen."

I said : " Nonsense, dear."

In the evening Lupin arrived home early, and seemed a little agitated. I said : " What's up, my boy ? " He hesitated a good deal, and then said : " You know those Parachikka Chlorates I advised you to invest £20 in ? " I replied : " Yes, they are all right, I trust ? " He replied : " Well, no ! To the surprise of everybody, they have utterly collapsed."

My breath was so completely taken away, I could say nothing. Carrie looked at me, and said : " What did I tell you ? " Lupin, after a while, said : "However, you are specially fortunate. I received an early tip, and sold out yours immediately, and was fortunate to get £2 for them. So you get something after all."

I gave a sigh of relief. I said : "I was not so sanguine as to suppose, as you predicted, that I should get six or eight times the amount of my investment ; still a profit of £2 is a good percentage for such a short time." Lupin said, quite irritably : "You don't understand. I sold your £20 shares for £2 ; you therefore lose £18 on the transaction, whereby Cummings and Gowing will lose the whole of theirs."

February 19. Lupin, before going to town, said : "I am very sorry about those Parachikka Chlorates ; it would not have happened if the boss, Job Cleanands, had been in town. Between ourselves, you must not be surprised if something goes wrong at our office. Job Cleanands has not been seen the last few days, and it strikes me several people *do* want to see him very particularly."

In the evening Lupin was just on the point of going out to avoid a collision with Gowing and Cummings, when the former entered the room, without knocking, but with his usual trick of saying, "May I come in ?"

He entered, and to the surprise of Lupin and myself, seemed to be in the very best of spirits. Neither Lupin nor I broached the subject to him, but he did so of his own accord. He said : "I say, those Parachikka Chlorates have gone an awful smash! You're a nice one, Master Lupin. How much do you lose?" Lupin, to my utter astonishment, said "Oh! I had nothing in them. There was some informality in my application— I forgot to enclose the cheque or something, and I didn't get any. The Guv. loses £18." I said: "I quite understood you were in it, or nothing would have induced me to speculate." Lupin replied: "Well, it can't be helped; you must go double on the next tip." Before I could reply, Gowing said: "Well, I lose nothing, fortunately. From what I heard, I did not quite believe in them, so I persuaded Cummings to take my £15 worth, as he had more faith in them than I had."

Lupin burst out laughing, and, in the most unseemly manner, said: "Alas, poor Cummings! He'll lose £35." At that moment there was a ring at the bell. Lupin said: "I don't want to meet Cummings." If he had gone out of the door he would have met him in the passage, so as quickly as possible Lupin opened the parlour window and got out. Gowing jumped up suddenly, exclaiming: "I don't want to see him either!" and, before I could say a word, he followed Lupin out of the window.

For my own part, I was horrified to think my own son and one of my most intimate friends should depart from the house like a couple of interrupted burglars. Poor Cummings was very upset, and of course was naturally very angry both with Lupin and Gowing. I pressed him to have a little whisky, and he replied that he had given up whisky; but would like a little "Unsweetened," as he was advised it was the most healthy spirit. I had none in the house, but sent Sarah round to Lockwood's for some.

February 20. The first thing that caught my eye on opening the *Standard* was—"Great Failure of Stock and Share Dealers! Mr. Job Cleanands Absconded!" I handed it to Carrie and she replied: "Oh! perhaps it's for Lupin's good. I never did think it a suitable situation for him." I thought the whole affair very shocking.

Lupin came down to breakfast, and seeing he looked painfully distressed, I said: "We know the news, my dear boy, and feel very sorry for you." Lupin said: "How did you know? Who told you?" I handed him the *Standard*. He threw the paper down, and said: "Oh I don't care a button for that! I expected that, but I did not expect this." He then read a letter from Frank Mutlar, announcing, in a cool manner, that Daisy Mutlar is to be married next month to Murray Posh. I exclaimed, "Murray Posh! Is not that the very man Frank had the impudence to bring here last Tuesday week?" Lupin said: "Yes; the '*Posh's-three-shilling-hats*' chap."

We all then ate our breakfast in dead silence. In fact, I could eat nothing. I was not only too worried, but I cannot and will not eat cushion of bacon. If I cannot get streaky bacon, I will do without anything.

When Lupin rose to go I noticed a malicious smile creep over his face. I asked him what it meant. He replied: "Oh! only a little consolation—still it *is* a consolation. I have just remembered that, by *my* advice, Mr. Murray Posh has invested £600 in Parachikka Chlorates!"

MARRIAGE OF DAISY MUTLAR AND MURRAY POSH. THE DREAM OF MY LIFE REALISED. MR. PERKUPP TAKES LUPIN INTO THE OFFICE.

CHAPTER XVII

To-DAY being the day on which
March 20. Daisy Mutlar and Mr. Murray Posh
are to be married, Lupin has gone
with a friend to spend the day at Gravesend.
Lupin has been much cut-up over the affair,
although he declares that he is glad it is off. I wish
he would not go to so many music-halls, but one
dare not say anything to him about it. At the
present moment he irritates me by singing all over
the house some nonsense about " What's the matter
with Gladstone? He's all right! What's the
matter with Lupin? He's all right! " *I* don't
think either of them is. In the evening Gowing
called, and the chief topic of conversation was
Daisy's marriage to Murray Posh. I said I
was glad the matter was at an end, as Daisy would
only have made a fool of Lupin. Gowing, with
his usual good taste, said : " Oh, Master Lupin
can make a fool of himself without any assistance."
Carrie very properly resented this, and Gowing
had sufficient sense to say he was sorry.

To-day I shall conclude my diary, for
March 21. it is one of the happiest days of my
life. My great dream of the last
few weeks—in fact, of many years—has been

realised. This morning came a letter from Mr. Perkupp, asking me to take Lupin down to the office with me. I went to Lupin's room; poor fellow, he seemed very pale, and said he had a bad headache. He had come back yesterday from Gravesend, where he spent part of the day in a small boat on the water, having been mad enough to neglect to take his overcoat with him. I showed him Mr. Perkupp's letter, and he got up as quickly as possible. I begged of him not to put on his fast-coloured clothes and ties, but to dress in something black or quiet-looking.

Carrie was all of a tremble when she read the letter, and all she could keep on saying was: "Oh, I *do* hope it will be all right." For myself, I could scarcely eat any breakfast. Lupin came down dressed quietly, and looking a perfect gentleman, except that his face was rather yellow. Carrie, by way of encouragement said: "You do look nice, Lupin." Lupin replied: "Yes, it's a good make-up, isn't it? A regular-downright-respectable-funereal-first-class-City-firm-junior-clerk." He laughed rather ironically.

In the hall I heard a great noise, and also Lupin shouting to Sarah to fetch down his old hat. I went into the passage, and found Lupin in a fury, kicking and smashing a new tall hat. I said: "Lupin, my boy, what are you doing? How wicked of you! Some poor fellow would be glad to have it." Lupin replied: "I would not insult any poor fellow by giving it to him."

When he had gone outside, I picked up the

battered hat, and saw inside "Posh's Patent."
Poor Lupin! I can forgive him. It seemed
hours before we reached the office. Mr. Perkupp
sent for Lupin, who was with him nearly an hour.
He returned, as I thought, crestfallen in appearance.
I said : " Well, Lupin, how about Mr. Perkupp ? "
Lupin commenced his song : "What's the
matter with Perkupp ? He's all right ! " I felt
instinctively my boy was engaged. I went to
Mr. Perkupp, but I could not speak. He said :
" Well, Mr. Pooter, what is it ? " I must have
looked a fool, for all I could say was : " Mr.
Perkupp, you are a good man." He looked at me
for a moment, and said : " No, Mr. Pooter, *you*
are the good man ; and we'll see if we cannot
get your son to follow such an excellent example."
I said : " Mr. Perkupp, may I go home ? I
cannot work any more to-day."

My good master shook my hand warmly as
he nodded his head. It was as much as I could
do to prevent myself from crying in the 'bus ;
in fact, I should have done so, had my thoughts
not been interrupted by Lupin, who was having
a quarrel with a fat man in the 'bus, whom he
accused of taking up too much room.

In the evening Carrie sent round for dear old
friend Cummings and his wife, and also to Gowing.
We all sat round the fire, and in a bottle of
" Jackson Frères," which Sarah fetched from the
grocer's, drank Lupin's health. I lay awake for
hours, thinking of the future. My boy in the
same office as myself—we can go down together

by the 'bus, come home together, and who knows but in the course of time he may take great interest in our little home. That he may help me to put a nail in here or a nail in there, or help his dear mother to hang a picture. In the summer he may help us in our little garden with the flowers, and assist us to paint the stands and pots. (By-the-by, I must get in some more enamel paint.) All this I thought over and over again, and a thousand happy thoughts beside. I heard the clock strike four, and soon after fell asleep, only to dream of three happy people—Lupin, dear Carrie, and myself.

TROUBLE WITH A STYLOGRAPHIC PEN.   WE
GO TO A VOLUNTEER BALL, WHERE I AM
LET IN FOR AN EXPENSIVE SUPPER.
GROSSLY INSULTED BY A CABMAN.   AN
ODD INVITATION TO SOUTHEND.

CHAPTER XVIII

April 8. No events of any importance, except that Gowing strongly recommended a new patent stylographic pen, which cost me nine-and-sixpence, and which was simply nine-and-sixpence thrown in the mud. It has caused me constant annoyance and irritability of temper. The ink oozes out of the top, making a mess on my hands, and once at the office when I was knocking the palm of my hand on the desk to jerk the ink down, Mr. Perkupp, who had just entered, called out: " Stop that knocking ! I suppose that is you, Mr. Pitt ? " That young monkey, Pitt, took a malicious glee in responding quite loudly : " No, sir ; I beg pardon, it is Mr. Pooter with his pen ; it has been going on all the morning." To make matters worse, I saw Lupin laughing behind his desk. I thought it wiser to say nothing. I took the pen back to the shop and asked them if they would take it back, as it did not act. I did not expect the full price returned, but was willing to take half. The man said he could not do that—buying and selling were two different things. Lupin's conduct during the period he has been in Mr. Perkupp's office has been most exemplary. My only fear is, it is too good to last.

Gowing called, bringing with him an
April 9.   invitation for Carrie and myself to a
ball given by the East Acton Rifle
Brigade, which he thought would be a swell affair,
as the member for East Acton (Sir William Grime)
had promised his patronage. We accepted of his
kindness, and he stayed to supper, an occasion I
thought suitable for trying a bottle of the sparkling
Algéra that Mr. James (of Sutton) had sent as a
present. Gowing sipped the wine, observing that
he had never tasted it before, and further remarked
that his policy was to stick to more recognised
brands. I told him it was a present from a dear
friend, and one mustn't look a gift-horse in the
mouth. Gowing facetiously replied : " And he
didn't like putting it in the mouth either."

I thought the remarks were rude without being
funny, but on tasting it myself, came to the
conclusion there was some justification for them.
The sparkling Algéra is very like cider, only more
sour. I suggested that perhaps the thunder had
turned it a bit acid. He merely replied : " Oh !
I don't think so." We had a very pleasant game of
cards, though I lost four shillings and Carrie lost
one, and Gowing said he had lost about sixpence :
how *he* could have lost, considering that Carrie and
I were the only other players, remains a mystery.

Owing, I presume, to the unsettled
April 14,   weather, I awoke with a feeling that my
Sunday.   skin was drawn over my face as tight
as a drum. Walking round the garden

with Mr. and Mrs. Treane, members of our congregation who had walked back with us, I was much annoyed to find a large newspaper full of bones on the gravel-path, evidently thrown over by those young Griffin boys next door ; who, whenever we have friends, climb up the empty steps inside their conservatory, tap at the windows, making faces, whistling, and imitating birds.

April 15. Burnt my tongue most awfully with the Worcester sauce, through that stupid girl Sarah shaking the bottle violently before putting it on the table.

April 16. The night of the East Acton Volunteer Ball. On my advice, Carrie put on the same dress that she looked so beautiful in at the Mansion House, for it had occurred to me, being a military ball, that Mr. Perkupp, who, I believe, is an officer in the Honorary Artillery Company, would in all probability be present. Lupin, in his usual incomprehensible language, remarked that he had heard it was a " bounders' ball." I didn't ask him what he meant though I didn't understand. Where he gets these expressions from I don't know ; he certainly doesn't learn them at home.

The invitation was for half-past eight, so I concluded if we arrived an hour later we should be in good time, without being " unfashionable," as Mrs. James says. It was very difficult to find— the cabman having to get down several times to

Young Griffin boys making faces, whistling and imitating birds.

inquire at different public-houses where the Drill Hall was. I wonder at people living in such out-of-the-way places. No one seemed to know it. However, after going up and down a good many badly-lighted streets we arrived at our destination. I had no idea it was so far from Holloway. I gave the cabman five shillings, who only grumbled, saying it was dirt cheap at half-a-sovereign, and was impertinent enough to advise me the next time I went to a ball to take a 'bus.

Captain Welcut received us, saying we were rather late, but that it was better late then never. He seemed a very good-looking gentleman though, as Carrie remarked, " rather short for an officer." He begged to be excused for leaving us, as he was engaged for a dance, and hoped we should make ourselves at home. Carrie took my arm and we walked round the rooms two or three times and watched the people dancing. I couldn't find a single person I knew, but attributed it to most of them being in uniform. As we were entering the supper-room I received a slap on the shoulder, followed by a welcome shake of the hand. I said: " Mr. Padge, I believe? " He replied: "That's right."

I gave Carrie a chair, and seated by her was a lady who made herself at home with Carrie at once.

There was a very liberal repast on the tables, plenty of champagne, claret, etc., and, in fact, everything seemed to be done regardless of expense. Mr. Padge is a man that, I admit, I have no particular liking for, but I felt so glad to come

across someone I knew, that I asked him to sit at
our table, and I must say that for a short fat man he
looked well in uniform, although I think his tunic
was rather baggy in the back. It was the only
supper-room that I have been in that was not
over-crowded ; in fact we were the only people
there, everybody being so busy dancing.

I assisted Carrie and her newly-formed
acquaintance, who said her name was Lupkin,
to some champagne ; also myself, and handed the
bottle to Mr. Padge to do likewise, saying : "You
must look after yourself." He replied : "That's
right," and poured out half a tumbler and drank
Carrie's health, coupled, as he said, "with her
worthy lord and master." We all had some
splendid pigeon pie, and ices to follow.

The waiters were very attentive, and asked if we
would like some more wine. I assisted Carrie and
her friend and Mr. Padge, also some people who
had just come from the dancing-room, who were
very civil. It occurred to me at the time that
perhaps some of the gentlemen knew me in the
City, as they were so polite. I made myself useful,
and assisted several ladies to ices, remembering an
old saying that "There is nothing lost by civility."

The band struck up for the dance, and they all
went into the ball-room. The ladies (Carrie and
Mrs. Lupkin) were anxious to see the dancing, and
as I had not quite finished my supper, Mr. Padge
offered his arms to them and escorted them to
the ball-room, telling me to follow. I said to
Mr. Padge : "It is quite a West End affair,"

to which remark Mr. Padge replied : " That's right."

When I had quite finished my supper, and was leaving, the waiter who had been attending on us arrested my attention by tapping me on the shoulder. I thought it unusual for a waiter at a private ball to expect a tip, but nevertheless gave a shilling, as he had been very attentive. He smilingly replied : " I beg your pardon, sir, this is no good," alluding to the shilling. " Your party's had four suppers at 5s. a head, five ices at 1s., three bottles of champagne at 11s. 6d., a glass of claret, and a sixpenny cigar for the stout gentleman —in all £3 0s. 6d. ! "

I don't think I was ever so surprised in my life, and had only sufficient breath to inform him that I had received a private invitation, to which he answered that he was perfectly well aware of that ; but that the invitation didn't include eatables and drinkables. A gentleman who was standing at the bar corroborated the waiter's statement, and assured me it was quite correct.

The waiter said he was extremely sorry if I had been under any misapprehension ; but it was not his fault. Of course there was nothing to be done but to pay. So, after turning out my pockets, I just managed to scrape up sufficient, all but nine shillings ; but the manager, on my giving my card to him, said : " That's all right."

I don't think I ever felt more humiliated in my life, and I determined to keep this misfortune from Carrie, for it would entirely destroy the pleasant evening she was enjoying. I felt there was no more enjoyment for me that evening, and it being late, I sought Carrie and Mrs. Lupkin. Carrie said she was quite ready to go, and Mrs. Lupkin, as we were wishing her "Good-night," asked Carrie and myself if we ever paid a visit to Southend? On my replying that I hadn't been there for many years, she very kindly said: "Well, why don't you come down and stay at our place?" As her invitation was so pressing, and observing that Carrie wished to go, we promised we would visit her the next Saturday week, and stay till Monday. Mrs. Lupkin said she would write to us to-morrow, giving us the address and particulars of trains, etc.

When we got outside the Drill Hall it was raining so hard that the roads resembled canals, and I need hardly say we had great difficulty in getting a cabman to take us to Holloway. After waiting a bit, a man said he would drive us, anyhow, as far as "The Angel," at Islington, and we could easily get another cab from there. It was a tedious journey; the rain was beating against the windows and trickling down the inside of the cab.

When we arrived at "The Angel" the horse seemed tired out. Carrie got out and ran into a doorway, and when I came to pay, to my absolute horror I remembered I had no money, nor had Carrie. I explained to the cabman how we were situated. Never in my life have I ever been so insulted; the cabman, who was a rough bully and to my thinking not sober, called me every name he could lay his tongue to, and positively seized me by the beard, which he pulled till the tears came into my eyes. I took the number of a policeman (who witnessed the assault) for not taking the man in charge. The policeman said he couldn't interfere, that he had seen no assault, and that people should not ride in cabs without money.

We had to walk home in the pouring rain, nearly two miles, and when I got in I put down the conversation I had with the cabman, word for word, as I intend writing to the *Telegraph* for the purpose of proposing that cabs should be driven only by men under Government control, to prevent civilians being subjected to the disgraceful insult and outrage that I had had to endure.

April 17. No water in our cistern again. Sent for Putley, who said he would soon remedy that, the cistern being zinc.

April 18. Water all right again in the cistern. Mrs. James, of Sutton, called in the afternoon. She and Carrie draped the mantelpiece in the drawing-room, and put little toy spiders, frogs and beetles all over it, as Mrs. James says it's quite the fashion. It was Mrs. James' suggestion, and of course Carrie always does what Mrs. James suggests. For my part, I preferred the mantelpiece as it was ; but there, I'm a plain man, and don't pretend to be in the fashion.

H

April 19. Our next-door neighbour, Mr. Griffin, called, and in a rather offensive tone accused me, or " someone," of boring a hole in his cistern and letting out his water to supply our cistern, which adjoined his. He said he should have his repaired, and send us in the bill.

April 20. Cummings called, hobbling in with a stick, saying he had been on his back for a week. It appears he was trying to shut his bedroom door, which is situated just at the top of the staircase, and unknown to him a piece of cork the dog had been playing with had got between the door, and prevented it shutting ; and in pulling the door hard, to give it an extra slam, the handle came off in his hands, and he fell backwards downstairs.

On hearing this, Lupin suddenly jumped up from the couch and rushed out of the room sideways. Cummings looked very indignant, and remarked it was very poor fun a man nearly breaking his back ; and though I had my suspicions that Lupin was laughing, I assured Cummings that he had only run out to open the door to a friend he expected. Cummings said this was the second time he had been laid up, and we had never sent to inquire. I said I knew nothing about it. Cummings said : " It was mentioned in the *Bicycle News*."

April 22. I have of late frequently noticed Carrie rubbing her nails a good deal with an instrument, and on asking her what she was doing, she replied : " Oh, I'm going in for manicuring. It's all the fashion now." I said : " I suppose Mrs. James introduced that into your head." Carrie laughingly replied : " Yes ; but everyone does it now."

I wish Mrs. James wouldn't come to the house. Whenever she does she always introduces some new-fangled rubbish into Carrie's head. One of these days I feel sure I shall tell her she's not welcome. I am sure it was Mrs. James who put Carrie up to writing on dark slate-coloured paper with white ink. Nonsense !

April 23.   Received a letter from Mrs. Lupkin, of Southend, telling us the train to come by on Saturday, and hoping we will keep our promise to stay with her. The letter concluded : " You must come and stay at our house ; we shall charge you half what you will have to pay at the Royal, and the view is every bit as good." Looking at the address at the top of the note-paper, I found it was : " Lupkin's Family and Commercial Hotel."

I wrote a note, saying we were compelled to " decline her kind invitation." Carrie thought this very satirical, and to the point.

By-the-by, I will never choose another cloth pattern at night. I ordered a new suit of dittos for the garden at Edwards', and chose the pattern by gaslight, and they seemed to be a quiet pepper-and-salt mixture with white stripes down. They came home this morning, and, to my horror, I found it was quite a flash-looking suit. There was a lot of green with bright yellow-coloured stripes.

I tried on the coat, and was annoyed to find Carrie giggling. She said : " What mixture did you say you asked for ? "

I said : " A quiet pepper-and-salt."

Carrie said : " Well, it looks more like mustard, if you want to know the truth."

MEET TEDDY FINSWORTH, AN OLD
SCHOOLFELLOW. WE HAVE A PLEASANT
AND QUIET DINNER AT HIS UNCLE'S,
MARRED ONLY BY A FEW AWKWARD
MISTAKES ON MY PART RESPECTING MR.
FINSWORTH'S PICTURES. A DISCUSSION
ON DREAMS.

CHAPTER XIX

Kept a little later than usual at the April 27. office, and as I was hurrying along a man stopped me, saying : " Hulloh ! That's a face I know." I replied politely : " Very likely ; lots of people know *me*, although I may not know them." He replied : " But you know *me*—Teddy Finsworth." So it was. He was at the same school with me. I had not seen him for years and years. No wonder I did not know him ! At school he was at least a head taller than I was ; now I am at least a head taller than he is, and he has a thick beard, almost grey. He insisted on my having a glass of wine (a thing I never do), and told me he lived at Middlesboro', where he was Deputy Town Clerk, a position which was as high as the Town Clerk of London—in fact, higher. He added that he was staying for a few days in London, with his uncle, Mr. Edgar Paul Finsworth (of Finsworth and Pultwell). He said he was sure his uncle would be only too pleased to see me, and he had a nice house, Watney Lodge, only a few minutes' walk from Muswell Hill Station. I gave him our address, and we parted.

In the evening, to my surprise, he called with a very nice letter from Mr. Finsworth, saying if we (including Carrie) would dine with them to-morrow (Sunday), at two o'clock, he would

be delighted.   Carrie did not like to go ; but
Teddy Finsworth pressed us so much we consented.   Carrie sent Sarah round to the butcher's
and countermanded our half-leg of mutton, which
we had ordered for to-morrow.

April 28,
Sunday.

We found Watney Lodge farther off
than we anticipated, and only arrived
as the clock struck two, both feeling
hot and uncomfortable.   To make
matters worse, a large collie dog pounced forward
to receive us.   He barked loudly and jumped up
at Carrie, covering her light skirt, which she was
wearing for the first time, with mud.   Teddy
Finsworth came out and drove the dog off and
apologised.   We were shown into the drawing-
room, which was beautifully decorated.   It was
full of knick-knacks, and some plates hung up on
the wall.   There were several little wooden milk-
stools with paintings on them ;   also a white
wooden banjo, painted by one of Mr. Paul
Finsworth's nieces—a cousin of Teddy's.

Mr. Paul Finsworth seemed quite a distin-
guished-looking elderly gentleman, and was most
gallant to Carrie.   There were a great many
water-colours hanging on the walls, mostly
different views of India, which were very bright.
Mr. Finsworth said they were painted by " Simpz,"
and added that he was no judge of pictures himself
but had been informed on good authority that
they were worth some hundreds of pounds,
although he had only paid a few shillings apiece

for them, frames included, at a sale in the neighbourhood.

There was also a large picture in a very handsome frame, done in coloured crayons. It looked like a religious subject. I was very much struck with the lace collar, it looked so real, but I unfortunately made the remark that there was something about the expression of the face that was not quite pleasing. It looked pinched. Mr. Finsworth sorrowfully replied: "Yes, the face was done after death—my wife's sister."

I felt terribly awkward and bowed apologetically, and in a whisper said I hoped I had not hurt his feelings. We both stood looking at the picture for a few minutes in silence, when Mr. Finsworth took out a handkerchief and said: "She was sitting in our garden last summer," and blew his nose violently. He seemed quite affected, so I turned to look at something else and stood in front of a portrait of a jolly-looking middle-aged gentleman, with a red face and straw hat. I said to Mr. Finsworth: "Who is this jovial-looking gentleman? Life doesn't seem to trouble him much." Mr. Finsworth said: "No, it doesn't. *He is dead too*—my brother."

I was absolutely horrified at my own awkwardness. Fortunately at this moment Carrie entered with Mrs. Finsworth, who had taken her upstairs to take off her bonnet and brush her skirt. Teddy said: "Short is late," but at that moment the gentleman referred to arrived, and I was introduced to him by Teddy, who said: "Do you know

*H

"*He is dead too.*"

Mr. Short ? " I replied, smiling, that I had not that pleasure, but I hoped it would not be *long* before I knew Mr. *Short*. He evidently did not see my little joke, although I repeated it twice with a little laugh. I suddenly remembered it was Sunday, and Mr. Short was perhaps *very particular*.

In this I was mistaken, for he was not at all particular in several of his remarks after dinner. In fact I was so ashamed of one of his observations that I took the opportunity to say to Mrs. Finsworth that I feared she found Mr. Short occasionally a little embarrassing. To my surprise she said : " Oh ! he is privileged you know." I did *not* know as a matter of fact, and so I bowed apologetically. I fail to see why Mr. Short should be privileged.

Another thing that annoyed me at dinner was that the collie dog, which jumped up at Carrie, was allowed to remain under the dining-room table. It kept growling and snapping at my boots every time I moved my foot. Feeling nervous rather, I spoke to Mrs. Finsworth about the animal, and she remarked : " It is only his play." She jumped up and let in a frightfully ugly-looking spaniel called Bibbs, which had been scratching at the door. This dog also seemed to take a fancy to my boots, and I discovered afterwards that it had licked off every bit of blacking from them. I was positively ashamed of being seen in them. Mrs. Finsworth, who, I must say, is not much of a Job's comforter, said:

"Oh! we are used to Bibbs doing that to our visitors."

Mr. Finsworth had up some fine port, although I question whether it is a good thing to take on the top of beer. It made me feel a little sleepy, while it had the effect of inducing Mr. Short to become "privileged" to rather an alarming extent. It being cold even for April, there was a fire in the drawing-room; we sat around in easy-chairs, and Teddy and I waxed rather eloquent over the old school days, which had the effect of sending all the others to sleep. I was delighted, as far as Mr. Short was concerned, that it *did* have that effect on him.

We stayed till four, and the walk home was remarkable only for the fact that several fools giggled at the unpolished state of my boots. Polished them myself when I got home. Went to church in the evening, and could scarcely keep awake. I will not take port on the top of beer again.

April 29. I am getting quite accustomed to being snubbed by Lupin, and I do not mind being sat upon by Carrie, because I think she has a certain amount of right to do so; but I do think it hard to be at once snubbed by wife, son, and both my guests.

Gowing and Cummings had dropped in during the evening, and I suddenly remembered an extraordinary dream I had a few nights ago, and I thought I would tell them about it. I dreamt

I saw some huge blocks of ice in a shop with a bright glare behind them. I walked into the shop and the heat was overpowering. I found that the blocks of ice were on fire. The whole thing was so real and yet so supernatural I woke up in a cold perspiration. Lupin in a most contemptuous manner, said : " What utter rot ! "

Before I could reply, Gowing said there was nothing so completely uninteresting as other people's dreams.

I appealed to Cummings, but he said he was bound to agree with the others, and my dream was especially nonsensical. I said : " It seemed so real to me." Gowing replied : " Yes, to *you*, perhaps, but not to *us*." Whereupon they all roared.

Carrie, who had hitherto been quiet, said : " He tells me his stupid dreams every morning nearly." I replied : " Very well, dear, I promise you I will never tell you or anybody else another dream of mine the longest day I live." Lupin said : " Hear ! hear ! " and helped himself to another glass of beer. The subject was fortunately changed, and Cummings read a most interesting article on the superiority of the bicycle to the horse.

DINNER AT FRANCHING'S TO MEET MR. HARDFUR HUTTLE.

CHAPTER XX

Received a letter from Mr. Franching,
May 10. of Peckham, asking us to dine with
him to-night, at seven o'clock, to meet
Mr. Hardfur Huttle, a very clever writer for the
American papers. Franching apologised for the
short notice; but said he had at the last moment
been disappointed of two of his guests and regarded
us as old friends who would not mind filling up
the gap. Carrie rather demurred at the invitation;
but I explained to her that Franching was very
well off and influential, and we could not afford
to offend him. "And we are sure to get a good
dinner and a good glass of champagne." "Which
never agrees with you!" Carrie replied, sharply.
I regarded Carrie's observation as unsaid. Mr.
Franching asked us to wire a reply. As he had
said nothing about dress in the letter, I wired
back: "With pleasure. Is it full dress?" and by
leaving out our name, just got the message within
the sixpence.

Got back early to give time to dress, which
we received a telegram instructing us to do. I
wanted Carrie to meet me at Franching's house;
but she would not do so, so I had to go home to
fetch her. What a long journey it is from Holloway
to Peckham! Why do people live such a long
way off? Having to change 'buses, I allowed

plenty of time—in fact, too much ; for we arrived at twenty minutes to seven, and Franching, so the servant said, had only just gone up to dress. However, he was down as the clock struck seven ; he must have dressed very quickly.

I must say it was quite a distinguished party, and although we did not know anybody personally, they all seemed to be quite swells. Franching had got a professional waiter, and evidently spared no expense. There were flowers on the table round some fairy-lamps, and the effect, I must say, was exquisite. The wine was good and there was plenty of champagne, concerning which Franching said he, himself, never wished to taste better. We were ten in number, and a *menu* card to each. One lady said she always preserved the *menu* and got the guests to write their names on the back.

We all of us followed her example, except Mr. Huttle, who was of course the important guest.

The dinner-party consisted of Mr. Franching, Mr. Hardfur Huttle, Mr. and Mrs. Samuel Hillbutter, Mrs. Field, Mr. and Mrs. Purdick, Mr. Pratt, Mr. R. Kent, and, last but not least, Mr. and Mrs. Charles Pooter. Franching said he was sorry he had no lady for me to take in to dinner. I replied that I preferred it, which I afterwards thought was a very uncomplimentary observation to make.

I sat next to Mrs. Field at dinner. She seemed a well-informed lady, but was very deaf. It did not much matter, for Mr. Hardfur Huttle did all the talking. He is a marvellously intellectual man and says things which from other people would seem quite alarming. How I wish I could remember even a quarter of his brilliant conversation. I made a few little reminding notes on the *menu* card.

One observation struck me as being absolutely powerful—though not to my way of thinking of course. Mrs. Purdick happened to say : " You are certainly unorthodox, Mr. Huttle." Mr. Huttle, with a peculiar expression (I can see it now) said in a slow, rich voice : " Mrs. Purdick, ' orthodox ' is a grandiloquent word implying sticking-in-the-mud. If Columbus and Stephenson had been orthodox, there would neither have been the discovery of America nor the steam-engine." There was quite a silence. It appeared to me that such teaching was absolutely dangerous, and yet I felt—in fact we must all have felt—there was no answer to the argument. A little later on Mrs. Purdick, who is Franching's sister and also acted as hostess, rose from the table, and Mr. Huttle said : " Why, ladies, do you deprive us of your company so soon ? Why not wait while we have our cigars ? "

The effect was electrical. The ladies (including Carrie) were in no way inclined to be deprived of Mr. Huttle's fascinating society, and immediately resumed their seats, amid much laughter and a little chaff. Mr. Huttle said : " Well, that's a real good sign ; you shall not be insulted by being called orthodox any longer." Mrs. Purdick, who

W.G.

"' Orthodox ' is a grandiloquent word."

seemed to be a bright and rather sharp woman, said : " Mr. Huttle, we will meet you half-way— that is, till you get half-way through your cigar. That, at all events, will be the happy medium."

I shall never forget the effect the words, " happy medium," had upon him. He was brilliant and most daring in his interpretation of the words. He positively alarmed me. He said something like the following : " Happy medium, indeed. Do you know ' happy medium ' are two words which mean ' miserable mediocrity ' ? I say, go first class or third ; marry a duchess or her kitchen-maid. The happy medium means respectability, and respectability means insipidness. Does it not, Mr. Pooter ? "

I was so taken aback by being personally appealed to, that I could only bow apologetically, and say I feared I was not competent to offer an opinion. Carrie was about to say something ; but she was interrupted, for which I was rather pleased, for she is not clever at argument, and one has to be extra clever to discuss a subject with a man like Mr. Huttle.

He continued, with an amazing eloquence that made his unwelcome opinions positively convincing : " The happy medium is nothing more or less than a vulgar half-measure. A man who loves champagne and, finding a pint too little, fears to face a whole bottle and has recourse to an imperial pint, will never build a Brooklyn Bridge or an Eiffel Tower. No, he is half-hearted, he is a half-measure—respectable—in fact, a happy medium, and will spend the rest of his days in a suburban villa with a stucco-column portico, resembling a four-post bedstead."

We all laughed.

"That sort of thing," continued Mr. Huttle, "belongs to a soft man, with a soft beard, with a soft head, with a made tie that hooks on."

This seemed rather personal, and twice I caught myself looking in the glass of the chiffonier; for *I* had on a tie that hooked on—and why not? If these remarks were not personal they were rather careless, and so were some of his subsequent observations, which must have made both Mr. Franching and his guests rather uncomfortable. I don't think Mr. Huttle meant to be personal, for he added: "We don't know that class here in this country; but we do in America, and I've no use for them."

Franching several times suggested that the wine should be passed round the table, which Mr. Huttle did not heed; but continued as if he were giving a lecture:

"What we want in America is your homes. We live on wheels. Your simple, quiet life and home, Mr. Franching, are charming. No display, no pretension! You make no difference in your dinner, I dare say, when you sit down by yourself and when you invite us. You have your own personal attendant—no hired waiter to breathe on the back of your head."

I saw Franching palpably wince at this.

Mr. Huttle continued: "Just a small dinner

with a few good things, such as you have this evening. You don't insult your guests by sending to the grocer for champagne at six shillings a bottle."

I could not help thinking of " Jackson Frères " at three-and-six !

" In fact," said Mr. Huttle, " a man is little less than a murderer who does. That is the province of the milksop, who wastes his evening at home playing dominoes with his wife. I've heard of these people. We don't want them at this table. Our party is well selected. We've no use for deaf old women, who cannot follow intellectual conversation."

All our eyes were turned to Mrs. Field, who fortunately, being deaf, did not hear his remarks ; but continued smiling approval.

" We have no representative at Mr. Franching's table," said Mr. Huttle, " of the unenlightened frivolous matron, who goes to a second class dance at Bayswater and fancies she is in Society. Society does not know her ; it has no use for her."

Mr. Huttle paused for a moment, and the opportunity was afforded for the ladies to rise. I asked Mr. Franching quietly to excuse me, as I did not wish to miss the last train, which we very nearly did, by-the-by, through Carrie having mislaid the little cloth cricket-cap which she wears when we go out.

It was very late when Carrie and I got home ; but on entering the sitting-room I said : " Carrie, what do you think of Mr. Hardfur Huttle ? "

She simply answered : " How like Lupin ! " The same idea occurred to me in the train. The comparison kept me awake half the night. Mr. Huttle was, of course, an older and more influential man ; but he *was* like Lupin, and it made me think how dangerous Lupin would be if he were older and more influential. I feel proud to think Lupin *does* resemble Mr. Huttle in some ways. Lupin, like Mr. Huttle, has original and sometimes wonderful ideas ; but it is those ideas that are so dangerous. They make men extremely rich or extremely poor. They make or break men. I always feel people are happier who live a simple unsophisticated life. I believe *I* am happy because I am not ambitious. Somehow I feel that Lupin, since he has been with Mr. Perkupp, has become content to settle down and follow the footsteps of his father. This is a comfort.

LUPIN IS DISCHARGED. WE ARE IN GREAT
TROUBLE. LUPIN GETS ENGAGED
ELSEWHERE AT A HANDSOME SALARY.

CHAPTER XXI

A TERRIBLE misfortune has happened.
May 13. Lupin is discharged from Mr. Perkupp's
office, and I scarcely know how I am
writing my diary. I was away from office last
Sat., the first time I have been absent through
illness for twenty years. I believe I was poisoned
by some lobster. Mr. Perkupp was also absent,
as Fate would have it; and our most valued
customer, Mr. Crowbillon, went to the office in a
rage, and withdrew his custom. My boy Lupin
not only had the assurance to receive him, but
recommended him the firm of Gylterson, Sons
and Co. Limited. In my own humble judgment,
and though I have to say it against my own son,
this seems an act of treachery.

This morning I receive a letter from Perkupp,
informing me that Lupin's services are no longer
required, and an interview with me is desired
at eleven o'clock. I went down to the office with
an aching heart, dreading an interview with Mr.
Perkupp, with whom I have never had a word. I
saw nothing of Lupin in the morning. He had
not got up when it was time for me to leave, and
Carrie said I should do no good by disturbing him.
My mind wandered so at the office that I could not
do my work properly.

As I expected, I was sent for by Mr. Perkupp,

and the following conversation ensued as nearly as I can remember it.

Mr. Perkupp said: "Good-morning, Mr. Pooter! This is a very serious business. I am not referring so much to the dismissal of your son, for I knew we should have to part sooner or later. *I* am the head of this old, influential, and much-respected firm; and when *I* consider the time has come to revolutionise the business, *I* will do it myself."

I could see my good master was somewhat affected, and I said: "I hope, sir, you do not imagine that I have in any way countenanced my son's unwarrantable interference?" Mr. Perkupp rose from his seat and took my hand, and said: "Mr. Pooter, I would as soon suspect myself as suspect you." I was so agitated that in the confusion, to show my gratitude, I very nearly called him a "grand old man."

Fortunately I checked myself in time, and said he was a "grand old master." I was so unaccountable for my actions that I sat down, leaving him standing. Of course, I at once rose, but Mr. Perkupp bade me sit down, which I was very pleased to do. Mr. Perkupp, resuming, said: "You will understand, Mr. Pooter, that the high-standing nature of our firm will not admit of our bending to anybody. If Mr. Crowbillon chooses to put his work into other hands—I may add, less experienced hands—it is not for us to bend and beg back his custom." "You *shall* not do it, sir," I said with indignation. "Exactly," replied Mr.

Perkupp ; " I shall *not* do it. But I was thinking this, Mr. Pooter. Mr. Crowbillon is our most valued client, and I will even confess—for I know this will not go beyond ourselves—that we cannot afford very well to lose him, especially in these times, which are not of the brightest. Now, I fancy you can be of service."

I replied : " Mr. Perkupp, I will work day and night to serve you ! "

Mr. Perkupp said : " I know you will. Now, what I should like you to do is this. You yourself might write to Mr. Crowbillon—you must not, of course, lead him to suppose I know anything about your doing so—and explain to him that your son was only taken on as a clerk — quite an inexperienced one in fact—out of the respect the firm had for you, Mr. Pooter. This is, of course, a fact. I don't suggest that you should speak in too strong terms of your own son's conduct ; but I may add, that had he been a son of mine, I should have condemned his interference with no measured terms. That I leave to you. I think the result will be that Mr. Crowbillon will see the force of the foolish step he has taken, and our firm will neither suffer in dignity nor in pocket."

I could not help thinking what a noble gentleman Mr. Perkupp is. His manners and his way of speaking seem to almost thrill one with respect.

I said : " Would you like to see the letter before I send it ? ".

Mr. Perkupp said : " Oh no ! I had better not. I am supposed to know nothing about it, and I

have every confidence in you. You must write the
letter carefully. We are not very busy; you had
better take the morning to-morrow, or the whole
day if you like. I shall be here myself all day
to-morrow, in fact all the week, in case Mr.
Crowbillon should call."

I went home a little more cheerful, but I left
word with Sarah that I could not see either Gowing
or Cummings, nor in fact anybody, if they called in
the evening. Lupin came into the parlour for a
moment with a new hat on, and asked my opinion
of it. I said I was not in the mood to judge of hats,
and I did not think he was in a position to buy a
new one. Lupin replied carelessly: " I didn't
buy it; it was a present."

I have such terrible suspicions of Lupin now
that I scarcely like to ask him questions, as I
dread the answers so. He, however, saved me the
trouble.

He said: " I met a friend, an old friend, that I
did not quite think a friend at the time; but it's
all right. As he wisely said, ' all is fair in love and
war,' and there was no reason why we should not
be friends still. He's a jolly, good, all-round sort
of fellow, and a very different stamp from that
inflated fool of a Perkupp."

I said: " Hush, Lupin! Do not pray add insult
to injury."

Lupin said: " What do you mean by injury?
I repeat, I have done no injury. Crowbillon is
simply tired of a stagnant stick-in-the-mud firm,
and made the change on his own account. I

simply recommended the new firm as a matter of biz—good old biz ! "

I said quietly : " I don't understand your slang, and at my time of life have no desire to learn it ; so, Lupin, my boy, let us change the subject. I will, if it please you, *try* and be interested in your new hat adventure."

Lupin said : " Oh ! there's nothing much about it, except I have not once seen him since his marriage, and he said he was very pleased to see me, and hoped we should be friends. I stood a drink to cement the friendship, and he stood me a new hat—one of his own."

I said rather wearily : " But you have not told me your old friend's name ? "

Lupin said, with affected carelessness : " Oh ! didn't I ? Well, I will. It was *Murray Posh.*"

May 14. Lupin came down late, and seeing me at home all the morning, asked the reason of it. Carrie and I both agreed it was better to say nothing to him about the letter I was writing, so I evaded the question.

Lupin went out, saying he was going to lunch with Murray Posh in the City. I said I hoped Mr. Posh would provide him with a berth. Lupin went out laughing, saying : " I don't mind *wearing* Posh's one-priced hats, but I am not going to *sell* them." Poor boy, I fear he is perfectly hopeless.

It took me nearly the whole day to write to Mr. Crowbillon. Once or twice I asked Carrie for suggestions ; and although it seems ungrateful, her suggestions were none of them to the point, while one or two were absolutely idiotic. Of course I did not tell her so. I got the letter off, and took it down to the office for Mr. Perkupp to see, but he again repeated that he could trust me.

Gowing called in the evening, and I was obliged to tell him about Lupin and Mr. Perkupp; and, to my surprise, he was quite inclined to side with Lupin. Carrie joined in, and said she thought I was taking much too melancholy a view of it. Gowing produced a pint sample-bottle of Madeira, which had been given him, which he said would get rid of the blues. I dare say it would have done so if there had been more of it; but as Gowing helped himself to three glasses, it did not leave much for Carrie and me to get rid of the blues with.

May 15. A day of great anxiety, for I expected every moment a letter from Mr. Crowbillon. Two letters came in the evening—one for me, with "Crowbillon Hall" printed in large gold-and-red letters on the back of the envelope; the other for Lupin, which I felt inclined to open and read, as it had "Gylterson, Sons, and Co. Limited," which was the recommended firm. I trembled as I opened Mr. Crowbillon's letter. I wrote him sixteen pages, closely written; he wrote me less than sixteen lines.

His letter was: "Sir,—I totally disagree with you. Your son, in the course of five minutes'

conversation, displayed more intelligence than
your firm has done during the last five years.—
Yours faithfully, Gilbert E. Gillam O. Crowbillon."

What am I to do? Here is a letter that I dare
not show to Mr. Perkupp, and would not show to
Lupin for anything. The crisis had yet to come;
for Lupin arrived, and, opening his letter, showed
a cheque for £25 as a commission for the
recommendation of Mr. Crowbillon, whose custom
to Mr. Perkupp is evidently lost for ever.
Cummings and Gowing both called, and both took
Lupin's part. Cummings went so far as to say
that Lupin would make a name yet. I suppose I
was melancholy, for I could only ask: "Yes, but
what sort of a name?"

May 16. I told Mr. Perkupp the contents of the
letter in a modified form, but Mr.
Perkupp said: "Pray don't discuss the
matter; it is at an end. Your son will bring his
punishment upon himself." I went home in the
evening, thinking of the hopeless future of Lupin.
I found him in most extravagant spirits and in
evening dress. He threw a letter on the table for
me to read.

To my amazement, I read that Gylterson
and Sons had absolutely engaged Lupin at a
salary of £200 a year, with other advantages. I
read the letter through three times and thought it
must have been for me. But there it was—
Lupin Pooter—plain enough. I was silent. Lupin
said: "What price Perkupp now? You take my

I

tip, Guv.—' off ' with Perkupp and freeze on to
Gylterson, the firm of the future ! Perkupp's firm ?
The stagnant dummies have been standing still
for years, and now are moving back. I want to go
on. In fact I must go off, as I am dining with the
Murray Poshs to-night."

In the exuberance of his spirits he hit his hat
with his stick, gave a loud war " Whoo-oop,"
jumped over a chair, and took the liberty of
rumpling my hair all over my forehead, and
bounced out of the room, giving me no chance of
reminding him of his age and the respect which
was due to his parent. Gowing and Cummings
came in the evening, and positively cheered me up
with congratulations respecting Lupin.

Gowing said : " I always said he would get on,
and, take my word, he has more in his head than
we three put together."

Carrie said . " He is a second Hardfur Huttle."

MASTER PERCY EDGAR SMITH JAMES.
MRS. JAMES (OF SUTTON) VISITS US AGAIN
AND INTRODUCES " SPIRITUAL SÉANCES."

CHAPTER XXII

WE went to Sutton after dinner to
May 26, have meat-tea with Mr. and Mrs.
Sunday. James. I had no appetite, having
dined well at two, and the entire
evening was spoiled by little Percy—their only
son—who seems to me to be an utterly spoiled
child.

Two or three times he came up to me and
deliberately kicked my shins. He hurt me once
so much that the tears came into my eyes. I
gently remonstrated with him, and Mrs. James
said : " Please don't scold him ; I do not believe
in being too severe with young children. You
spoil their character."

Little Percy set up a deafening yell here, and
when Carrie tried to pacify him, he slapped her
face.

I was so annoyed, I said : " That is not my
idea of bringing up children, Mrs. James."

Mrs. James said : " People have different
ideas of bringing up children—even your son
Lupin is not the standard of perfection."

A Mr. Mezzini (an Italian, I fancy) here took
Percy in his lap. The child wriggled and kicked
and broke away from Mr. Mezzini, saying :
" I don't like you—you've got a dirty face."

Master Percy Edgar Smith James.

A very nice gentleman, Mr. Birks Spooner, took the child by the wrist and said : " Come here, dear, and listen to this."

He detached his chronometer from the chain and made his watch strike six.

To our horror, the child snatched it from his hand and bounced it down upon the ground like one would a ball.

Mr. Birks Spooner was most amiable, and said he could easily get a new glass put in, and did not suppose the works were damaged.

To show you how people's opinions differ, Carrie said the child was bad-tempered, but it made up for that defect by its looks, for it was— in her mind—an unquestionably beautiful child.

I may be wrong, but I do not think I have seen a much uglier child myself. That is *my* opinion.

May 30. I don't know why it is, but I never anticipate with any pleasure the visits to our house of Mrs. James, of Sutton. She is coming again to stay for a few days. I said to Carrie this morning, as I was leaving : " I wish, dear Carrie, I could like Mrs. James better than I do."

Carrie said : " So do I, dear ; but as for years I have had to put up with Mr. Gowing, who is vulgar, and Mr. Cummings, who is kind but most uninteresting, I am sure, dear, you won't mind the occasional visits of Mrs. James, who has more intellect in her little finger than both your friends have in their entire bodies."

I was so entirely taken aback by this onslaught on my two dear old friends, I could say nothing, and as I heard the 'bus coming, I left with a hurried kiss—a little too hurried, perhaps, for my upper lip came in contact with Carrie's teeth and slightly cut it. It was quite painful for an hour afterwards. When I came home in the evening I found Carrie buried in a book on Spiritualism, called *There is no Birth*, by Florence Singleyet. I need scarcely say the book was sent her to read by Mrs. James, of Sutton. As she had not a word to say outside her book, I spent the rest of the evening altering the stair-carpets, which are beginning to show signs of wear at the edges.

Mrs. James arrived and, as usual, in the evening took the entire management of everything. Finding that she and Carrie were making some preparations for table-turning, I thought it time really to put my foot down. I have always had the greatest contempt for such nonsense, and put an end to it years ago when Carrie, at our old house, used to have séances every night with poor Mrs. Fussters (who is now dead). If I could see any use in it, I would not care. As I stopped it in the days gone by I determined to do so now.

I said : " I am very sorry, Mrs. James, but I totally disapprove of it, apart from the fact that I receive my old friends on this evening."

Mrs. James said : " Do you mean to say you haven't read *There is no Birth* ? " I said : " No, and I have no intention of doing so." Mrs. James seemed surprised and said: " All the world is going mad over the book." I responded rather cleverly: " Let it. There will be one sane man in it, at all events."

Mrs. James said she thought I was very unkind, and if people were all as prejudiced as I was, there would never have been the electric telegraph or the telephone.

I said that was quite a different thing.

Mrs. James said sharply: " In what way, pray—in what way ? "

I said: " In many ways."

Mrs. James said: " Well, mention *one* way."

I replied quietly: " Pardon me, Mrs. James; I decline to discuss the matter. I am not interested in it."

Sarah at this moment opened the door and showed in Cummings, for which I was thankful, for I felt it would put a stop to this foolish table-turning. But I was entirely mistaken; for, on the subject being opened again, Cummings said he was most interested in Spiritualism, although he was bound to confess he did not believe much in it; still, he was willing to be convinced.

I firmly declined to take any part in it, with the result that my presence was ignored. I left the three sitting in the parlour at a small round table which they had taken out of the drawing-room. I walked into the hall with the ultimate intention of taking a little stroll. As I opened the door, who should come in but Gowing !

On hearing what was going on, he proposed

that we should join the circle and he would go into a trance. He added that he *knew* a few things about old Cummings, and would *invent* a few about Mrs. James. Knowing how dangerous Gowing is, I declined to let him take part in any such foolish performance. Sarah asked me if she could go out for half an hour, and I gave her permission, thinking it would be more comfortable to sit with Gowing in the kitchen than in the cold drawing-room. We talked a good deal about Lupin and Mr. and Mrs. Murray Posh, with whom he is as usual spending the evening. Gowing said : " I say, it wouldn't be a bad thing for Lupin if old Posh kicked the bucket."

My heart gave a leap of horror, and I rebuked Gowing very sternly for joking on such a subject. I lay awake half the night thinking of it—the other half was spent in nightmares on the same subject.

May 31. I wrote a stern letter to the laundress. I was rather pleased with the letter, for I thought it very satirical. I said : " You have returned the handkerchiefs without the colour. Perhaps you will return either the colour or the value of the handkerchiefs." I shall be rather curious to know what she will have to say.

More table-turning in the evening. Carrie said last night was in a measure successful, and they ought to sit again. Cummings came in, and seemed interested. I had the gas lighted in the drawing-room, got the steps, and repaired the cornice, which has been a bit of an eyesore to me. In a fit of unthinkingness—if I may use such an expression,—I gave the floor over the parlour, where the séance was taking place, two loud raps with the hammer. I felt sorry afterwards, for it was the sort of ridiculous, foolhardy thing that Gowing or Lupin would have done.

However, they never even referred to it, but Carrie declared that a message came through the table to her of a wonderful description, concerning someone whom she and I knew years ago, and who was quite unknown to the others.

When we went to bed, Carrie asked me as a favour to sit to-morrow night, to oblige her. She said it seemed rather unkind and unsociable on my part. I promised I would sit once.

June 1. I sat reluctantly at the table in the evening, and I am bound to admit some curious things happened. I contend they were coincidences, but they were curious. For instance, the table kept tilting towards me, which Carrie construed as a desire that I should ask the spirit a question. I obeyed the rules, and I asked the spirit (who said her name was Lina) if she could tell me the name of an old aunt of whom I was thinking, and whom we used to call Aunt Maggie. The table spelled out C A T. We could make nothing out of it, till I suddenly remembered that her second name was Catherine, which it was evidently trying to spell. I don't think even Carrie knew this. But if she did, she would never cheat. I must admit it was curious. Several other things happened, and I consented to sit at another séance on Monday.

June 3. The laundress called, and said she was very sorry about the handkerchiefs, and returned ninepence. I said, as the colour was completely washed out and the handkerchiefs quite spoiled, ninepence was not enough. Carrie replied that the two handkerchiefs originally only cost sixpence, for she remembered buying them at a sale at the Holloway *Bon Marché*. In that case, I insisted that threepence should be returned to the laundress. Lupin has gone to stay with the Poshs for a few days. I must say I feel very uncomfortable about it. Carrie said I was ridiculous to worry about it. Mr. Posh was very fond of Lupin, who, after all, was only a mere boy.

In the evening we had another séance, which, in some respects, was very remarkable, although the first part of it was a little doubtful. Gowing called, as well as Cummings, and begged to be allowed to join the circle. I wanted to object, but Mrs. James, who appears a good Medium (that is, if there is anything in it at all), thought there might be a little more spirit power if Gowing joined ; so the five of us sat down.

The moment I turned out the gas, and almost before I could get my hands on the table, it rocked violently and tilted, and began moving quickly across the room. Gowing shouted out : " Way, oh! steady, lad, steady!" I told Gowing if he could not behave himself I should light the gas, and put an end to the séance. To tell the truth, I thought Gowing was playing tricks, and I hinted as much; but Mrs. James said she had often seen the table go right off the ground. The spirit Lina came again, and said "WARN" three or four times, and declined to explain. Mrs. James said "Lina" was stubborn sometimes. She often behaved like that, and the best thing to do was to send her away.

She then hit the table sharply, and said: "Go away, Lina; you are disagreeable. Go away!" I should think we sat nearly three-quarters of an hour with nothing happening. My hands felt quite cold, and I suggested we should stop the séance. Carrie and Mrs. James, as well as Cummings, would not agree to it. In about ten minutes' time there was some tilting towards me. I gave the alphabet, and it spelled out S P O O F. As I have heard both Gowing and Lupin use the word, and as I could hear Gowing silently laughing, I directly accused him of pushing the table. He denied it; but, I regret to say, I did not believe him.

Gowing said: "Perhaps it means 'Spook,' a ghost."

I said: "*You* know it doesn't mean anything of the sort."

Gowing said: "Oh! very well—I'm sorry I 'spook,'" and he rose from the table.

No one took any notice of the stupid joke, and

Mrs. James suggested he should sit out for a while. Gowing consented and sat in the arm-chair.

The table began to move again, and we might have had a wonderful séance but for Gowing's stupid interruptions. In answer to the alphabet from Carrie the table spelt " NIPUL," then the " WARN " three times. We could not think what it meant till Cummings pointed out that " NIPUL " was Lupin spelled backwards. This was quite exciting. Carrie was particularly excited, and said she hoped nothing horrible was going to happen.

Mrs. James asked if " Lina " was the spirit. The table replied firmly, " No," and the spirit would not give his or her name. We then had the message, " NIPUL will be very rich."

Carrie said she felt quite relieved, but the word " WARN " was again spelt out. The table then began to oscillate violently, and in reply to Mrs. James, who spoke very softly to the table, the spirit began to spell its name. It first spelled " DRINK."

Gowing here said : " Ah ! that's more in my line."

I asked him to be quiet as the name might not be completed.

The table then spelt " WATER."

Gowing here interrupted again, and said : " Ah ! that's *not* in my line. *Outside* if you like, but not inside."

Carrie appealed to him to be quiet.

The table then spelt " CAPTAIN," and Mrs.

James startled us by crying out, "Captain Drinkwater, a very old friend of my father's, who has been dead some years."

This was more interesting, and I could not help thinking that after all there must be something in Spiritualism.

Mrs. James asked the spirit to interpret the meaning of the word "Warn" as applied to "NIPUL." The alphabet was given again, and we got the word "BOSH."

Gowing here muttered : "So it is."

Mrs. James said she did not think the spirit meant that, as Captain Drinkwater was a perfect gentleman, and would never have used the word in answer to a lady's question. Accordingly the alphabet was given again.

This time the table spelled distinctly "POSH." We all thought of Mrs. Murray Posh and Lupin. Carrie was getting a little distressed, and as it was getting late we broke up the circle.

We arranged to have one more to-morrow, as it will be Mrs. James' last night in town. We also determined *not* to have Gowing present.

Cummings, before leaving, said it was certainly interesting, but he wished the spirits would say something about him.

June 4.   Quite looking forward to the séance this evening. Was thinking of it all day at the office.

Just as we sat down at the table we were annoyed by Gowing entering without knocking.

He said : " I am not going to stop, but I have brought with me a sealed envelope, which I know I can trust with Mrs. Pooter. In that sealed envelope is a strip of paper on which I have asked a simple question. If the spirits can answer that question, I will believe in Spiritualism."

I ventured the expression that it might be impossible.

Mrs. James said : " Oh no ! it is of common occurrence for the spirits to answer questions under such conditions—and even for them to write on locked slates. It is quite worth trying. If ' Lina ' is in a good temper, she is certain to do it."

Gowing said : " All right ; then I shall be a firm believer. I shall perhaps drop in about half-past nine or ten, and hear the result."

He then left and we sat a long time. Cummings wanted to know something about some undertaking in which he was concerned, but he could get no answer of any description whatever—at which he said he was very disappointed and was afraid there was not much in table-turning after all. I thought this rather selfish of him. The séance was very similar to the one last night, almost the same in fact. So we turned to the letter. " Lina " took a long time answering the question, but eventually spelt out " ROSES, LILIES AND COWS." There was a great rocking of the table at this time, and Mrs. James said : " If that is Captain Drinkwater, let us ask him the answer as well ? "

It was the spirit of the Captain, and, most singular, he gave the same identical answer : " ROSES, LILIES, AND COWS."

I cannot describe the agitation with which Carrie broke the seal, or the disappointment we felt on reading the question, to which the answer was so inappropriate. The question was, " *What's old Pooter's age ?* "

This quite decided me.

As I had put my foot down on Spiritualism years ago, so I would again.

I am pretty easy-going as a rule, but I can be extremely firm when driven to it.

I said slowly, as I turned up the gas : " This is the last of this nonsense that shall ever take place under my roof. I regret I permitted myself to be a party to such tomfoolery. If there is anything in it—which I doubt—it is nothing of any good, and I *won't have it again*. That is enough."

Mrs. James said : " I think, Mr. Pooter, you are rather over-stepping —— "

I said : " Hush, madam. I am master of this house—please understand that."

Mrs. James made an observation which I sincerely hope I was mistaken in. I was in such a rage I could not quite catch what she said. But if I thought she said what it sounded like, she should never enter the house again.

LUPIN LEAVES US. WE DINE AT HIS NEW
APARTMENTS, AND HEAR SOME EXTRA-
ORDINARY INFORMATION RESPECTING THE
WEALTH OF MR. MURRAY POSH. MEET
MISS LILIAN POSH. AM SENT FOR BY
MR. HARDFUR HUTTLE. IMPORTANT.

CHAPTER XXIII

I FIND, on looking over my diary,
July 1. nothing of any consequence has taken
place during the last month. To-day
we lose Lupin, who has taken furnished apartments
at Bayswater, near his friends, Mr. and Mrs.
Murray Posh, at two guineas a week. I think this
is most extravagant of him, as it is half his salary.
Lupin says one never loses by a good address, and,
to use his own expression, Brickfield Terrace is a
bit " off." Whether he means it is " far off " I do
not know. I have long since given up trying to
understand his curious expressions. I said the
neighbourhood had always been good enough for
his parents. His reply was : " It is no question of
being good or bad. There is no money in it, and
I am not going to rot away my life in the suburbs."

We are sorry to lose him, but perhaps he will
get on better by himself, and there may be some
truth in his remark that an old and a young horse
can't pull together in the same cart.

Gowing called, and said that the house seemed
quite peaceful, and like old times. He liked Master
Lupin very well, but he occasionally suffered from
what he could not help—youth.

Cummings called, looked very pale, and
July 2. said he had been very ill again, and of
course not a single friend had been

near him. Carrie said she had never heard of it, whereupon he threw down a copy of the *Bicycle News* on the table, with the following paragraph : " We regret to hear that that favourite old roadster, Mr. Cummings ('Long' Cummings), has met with what might have been a serious accident in Rye Lane. A mischievous boy threw a stick between the spokes of one of the back wheels, and the machine overturned, bringing our brother tricyclist heavily to the ground. Fortunately he was more frightened than hurt, but we missed his merry face at the dinner at Chingford, where they turned up in good numbers. 'Long' Cummings' health was proposed by our popular Vice, Mr. Westropp, the prince of bicyclists, who in his happiest vein said it was a case of ' *Cumming*(s) thro' the *Rye*, but fortunately there was more *wheel* than *woe*,' a joke which created roars of laughter."

We all said we were very sorry, and pressed Cummings to stay to supper. Cummings said it was like old times being without Lupin, and he was much better away.

July 3, *Sunday*. In the afternoon, as I was looking out of the parlour window, which was open, a grand trap, driven by a lady, with a gentleman seated by the side of her, stopped at our door. Not wishing to be seen, I withdrew my head very quickly, knocking the back of it violently against the sharp edge of the window-sash. I was nearly stunned. There was a loud double-knock at the front door ; Carrie rushed out of the parlour, upstairs to her room, and I followed, as Carrie thought it was Mr. Perkupp. I thought it was Mr. Franching. I whispered to Sarah over the banisters : " Show them into the drawing-room." Sarah said, as the shutters were not opened, the room would smell musty. There was another loud rat-tat. I whispered : " Then show them into the parlour, and say Mr. Pooter will be down directly." I changed my coat, but could not see to do my hair, as Carrie was occupying the glass.

Sarah came up, and said it was Mrs. Murray Posh and Mr. Lupin.

This was quite a relief. I went down with Carrie, and Lupin met me with the remark : " I say, what did you run away from the window for ? Did we frighten you ? "

I foolishly said : " What window ? "

Lupin said : " Oh, you know. Shut it. You looked as if you were playing at Punch and Judy."

On Carrie asking if she could offer them anything, Lupin said : " Oh, I think Daisy will take on a cup of tea. I can do with a B. and S."

I said : " I am afraid we have no soda."

Lupin said : " Don't bother about that. You just trip out and hold the horse ; I don't think Sarah understands it."

They stayed a very short time, and as they were leaving, Lupin said : " I want you both to come and dine with me next Wednesday, and see my new place. Mr. and Mrs. Murray Posh, Miss Posh (Murray's sister) are coming. Eight o'clock sharp. No one else."

I said we did not pretend to be fashionable people, and would like the dinner earlier, as it made it so late before we got home.

Lupin said: "Rats! You must get used to it. If it comes to that, Daisy and I can drive you home."

We promised to go; but I must say in my simple mind the familiar way in which Mrs. Posh and Lupin addressed each other is reprehensible. Anybody would think they had been children together. I certainly should object to a six months' acquaintance calling *my* wife "Carrie," and driving out with her.

July 4. Lupin's rooms looked very nice; but the dinner was, I thought, a little too grand, especially as he commenced with champagne straight off. I also think Lupin might have told us that he and Mr. and Mrs. Murray Posh and Miss Posh were going to put on full evening dress. Knowing that the dinner was only for us six, we never dreamed it would be a full dress affair. I had no appetite. It was quite twenty minutes past eight before we sat down to dinner. At six I could have eaten a hearty meal. I had a bit of bread-and-butter at that hour, feeling famished, and I expect that partly spoiled my appetite.

We were introduced to Miss Posh, whom Lupin called "Lillie Girl," as if he had known her all his life. She was very tall, rather plain, and I thought she was a little painted round the eyes. I hope I am wrong; but she had such fair hair, and yet her eyebrows were black. She looked about thirty.

"*Lillie Girl.*"

I did not like the way she kept giggling and giving Lupin smacks and pinching him. Then her laugh was a sort of a scream that went right through my ears, all the more irritating because there was nothing to laugh at. In fact, Carrie and I were not at all prepossessed with her. They all smoked cigarettes after dinner, including Miss Posh, who startled Carrie by saying : " Don't you smoke, dear ? " I answered for Carrie, and said : " Mrs. Charles Pooter has not arrived at it yet," whereupon Miss Posh gave one of her piercing laughs again.

Mrs. Posh sang a dozen songs at least, and I can only repeat what I have said before—she does *not* sing in tune ; but Lupin sat by the side of the piano, gazing into her eyes the whole time. If I had been Mr. Posh, I think I should have had something to say about it. Mr. Posh made himself very agreeable to us, and eventually sent us home in his carriage, which I thought most kind. He is evidently very rich, for Mrs. Posh had on some beautiful jewellery. She told Carrie her necklace, which her husband gave her as a birthday present, alone cost £300.

Mr. Posh said he had a great belief in Lupin, and thought he would make rapid way in the world.

I could not help thinking of the £600 Mr. Posh lost over the *Parachikka Chlorates* through Lupin's advice.

During the evening I had an opportunity to speak to Lupin, and expressed a hope that Mr. Posh was not living beyond his means.

Lupin sneered, and said Mr. Posh was worth

thousands. "Posh's one-price hat" was a household word in Birmingham, Manchester, Liverpool, and all the big towns throughout England. Lupin further informed me that Mr. Posh was opening branch establishments at New York, Sydney, and Melbourne, and was negotiating for Kimberley and Johannesburg.

I said I was pleased to hear it.

Lupin said : " Why, he has settled over £10,000 on Daisy, and the same amount on ' Lillie Girl.' If at any time I wanted a little capital, he would put up a couple of ' thou ' at a day's notice, and could buy up Perkupp's firm over his head at any moment with ready cash."

On the way home in the carriage, for the first time in my life, I was inclined to indulge in the radical thought that money was *not* properly divided.

On arriving home at a quarter-past eleven, we found a hansom cab, which had been waiting for me for two hours with a letter. Sarah said she did not know what to do, as we had not left the address where we had gone. I trembled as I opened the letter, fearing it was some bad news about Mr. Perkupp. The note was : " Dear Mr. Pooter,— Come down to the Victoria Hotel without delay. Important. Yours truly, Hardfur Huttle."

I asked the cabman if it was too late. The cabman replied that it was *not ;* for his instructions were, if I happened to be out, he was to wait till I came home. I felt very tired, and really wanted to go to bed. I reached the hotel at a quarter before midnight. I apologised for being so late, but Mr. Huttle said: "Not at all; come and have a few oysters." I feel my heart beating as I write these words. To be brief, Mr. Huttle said he had a rich American friend who wanted to do something large in our line of business, and that Mr. Franching had mentioned my name to him. We talked over the matter. If, by any happy chance, the result be successful, I can more than compensate my dear master for the loss of Mr. Crowbillon's custom. Mr. Huttle had previously said: "The glorious 'Fourth' is a lucky day for America, and, as it has not yet struck twelve, we will celebrate it with a glass of the best wine to be had in the place, and drink good luck to our bit of business."

I fervently hope it will bring good luck to us all.

It was two o'clock when I got home. Although I was so tired, I could not sleep except for short intervals—then only to dream.

I kept dreaming of Mr. Perkupp and Mr. Huttle. The latter was in a lovely palace with a crown on. Mr. Perkupp was waiting in the room. Mr. Huttle kept taking off this crown and handing it to me, and calling me "President."

He appeared to take no notice of Mr. Perkupp, and I kept asking Mr. Huttle to give the crown to my worthy master. Mr. Huttle kept saying: "No, this is the White House of Washington, and you must keep your crown, Mr. President."

We all laughed long and very loudly, till I got parched, and then I woke up. I fell asleep, only to dream the same thing over and over again.

ONE OF THE HAPPIEST DAYS
OF MY LIFE.

CHAPTER THE LAST

July 10. THE excitement and anxiety through which I have gone the last few days have been almost enough to turn my hair grey. It is all but settled. To-morrow the die will be cast. I have written a long letter to Lupin—feeling it my duty to do so,—regarding his attention to Mrs. Posh, for they drove up to our house again last night.

July 11. I find my eyes filling with tears as I pen the note of my interview this morning with Mr. Perkupp. Addressing me, he said : "My faithful servant, I will not dwell on the important service you have done our firm. You can never be sufficiently thanked. Let us change the subject. Do you like your house, and are you happy where you are ? "

I replied : "Yes, sir ; I love my house and I love the neighbourhood, and could not bear to leave it."

Mr. Perkupp, to my surprise, said : "Mr. Pooter, I will purchase the freehold of that house, and present it to the most honest and most worthy man it has ever been my lot to meet."

He shook my hand, and said he hoped my wife and I would be spared many years to enjoy it. My heart was too full to thank him ; and, seeing

my embarrassment, the good fellow said : " You
need say nothing, Mr. Pooter," and left the office.

I sent telegrams to Carrie, Gowing, and
Cummings (a thing I have never done before),
and asked the two latter to come round to supper.

On arriving home I found Carrie crying with
joy, and I sent Sarah round to the grocer's to get
two bottles of " Jackson Frères."

My two dear friends came in the evening, and
the last post brought a letter from Lupin in reply
to mine. I read it aloud to them all. It ran :
" My dear old Guv.,—Keep your hair on. You
are on the wrong tack again. I am engaged to be
married to ' Lillie Girl.' I did not mention it last
Thursday, as it was not definitely settled. We
shall be married in August, and amongst our
guests we hope to see your old friends Gowing and
Cummings. With much love to all, from *The
same old Lupin.*"

THE END.